THE SPY

THE SPY

A NOVEL

Paulo Coelho

Translated from the Portuguese
by Zoë Perry

ALFRED A. KNOPF   New York
2016

THIS IS A BORZOI BOOK
PUBLISHED BY ALFRED A. KNOPF

Translation copyright © 2016 by Zoë Perry

All rights reserved. Published in the United States by
Alfred A. Knopf, a division of Penguin Random House LLC,
New York, and distributed in Canada by Random House
of Canada, a division of Penguin Random House Canada
Limited, Toronto. Originally published in Brazil as *A Espiã*
by Editora Paralela, a division of Editora Schwarcz S.A.,
São Paulo, in 2016. Copyright © 2016 by Paulo Coelho.
This edition published by arrangement with Sant Jordi
Asociados Agencia Literaria SLU, Barcelona, Spain.

www.aaknopf.com

Knopf, Borzoi Books, and the colophon are registered
trademarks of Penguin Random House LLC.

Library of Congress Control Number: 201695146
ISBN 9781524732066 (hardcover)   ISBN 9781524732073 (ebook)
ISBN 9781524711085 (open market)

Jacket design by Stephanie Ross

Photographs of Mata Hari herein are courtesy of the Collection
Fries Museum, Leeuwarden, The Netherlands. Image of the letter
on page 188 is courtesy of the National Archives, United Kingdom.

Manufactured in the United States of America
Published November 22, 2016
Second Printing Before Publication

O Mary,

conceived without sin,

pray for us who have recourse to You.

Amen.

"When thou goest with thine adversary to the magistrate, as thou art in the way, give diligence that thou mayest be delivered from him; lest he hale thee to the judge, and the judge deliver thee to the officer, and the officer cast thee into prison.

"I tell thee, thou shalt not depart thence, till thou hast paid the very last mite."

—LUKE 12:58–59

Based on real events

Prologue

PARIS, OCTOBER 15, 1917—
ANTON FISHERMAN AND HENRY WALES,
FOR THE INTERNATIONAL NEWS SERVICE

Shortly before 5 a.m., a party of eighteen men—most of them officers of the French army—climbed to the second floor of Saint-Lazare, the women's prison in Paris. Guided by a warder carrying a torch to light the lamps, they stopped in front of cell 12.

Nuns were charged with looking after the prison. Sister Leonide opened the door and asked that everyone wait outside as she entered the cell, struck a match against the wall, and lit the lamp inside. Then she called one of the other sisters to help.

With great affection and care, Sister Leonide draped her arm around the sleeping body. The woman struggled to waken, as though disinterested in anything. According to the nun's statement, when she finally awoke, it was as though she emerged from a peaceful slumber. She remained serene when she learned her appeal for clemency, made days earlier to the president of the republic, had been denied. It was impossible to decipher if she felt sadness or a sense of relief that everything was coming to an end.

On Sister Leonide's signal, Father Arbaux entered her cell along with Captain Bouchardon and her lawyer, Maître Clunet. The prisoner handed her lawyer the long letter that she had spent the previous week writing, as well as two manila envelopes containing news clippings.

She drew on black stockings, which seemed grotesque under the circumstances, and stepped into a pair of high-heeled shoes adorned with silk laces. As she rose from the bed, she reached for the hook in the corner of her cell, where a floor-length fur coat hung, its sleeves and collar trimmed with the fur of another animal, possibly fox. She slipped it over the heavy silk kimono in which she had slept.

Her black hair was disheveled. She brushed it carefully, then secured it at the nape of her neck. She perched a felt hat on top of her head and tied it under her chin with a silk ribbon, so the wind would not blow it out of place when she stood in the clearing where she was to be led.

Slowly, she bent down to take a pair of black leather gloves. Then, nonchalantly, she turned to the newcomers and said in a calm voice:

"I am ready."

Everyone departed the Saint-Lazare prison cell and headed toward the automobile that waited, its engine running, to take them to the firing squad.

The car sped through the streets of the sleeping city on its way to the Caserne de Vincennes barracks. A fort had stood there once, before being destroyed by the Germans in 1870.

Twenty minutes later, the automobile stopped and its party descended. Mata Hari was the last to exit.

The soldiers were already lined up for the execution. Twelve Zouaves formed the firing squad. At the end of the group stood an officer, his sword drawn.

Flanked by two nuns, Father Arbaux spoke with the condemned woman until a French lieutenant approached and held out a white cloth to one of the sisters, saying:

"Blindfold her eyes, please."

"Must I wear that?" asked Mata Hari, as she looked at the cloth.

Maître Clunet turned to the lieutenant questioningly.

"If Madame prefers not to, it is not mandatory," replied the lieutenant.

Mata Hari was neither bound nor blindfolded; she stood, gazing steadfastly at her executioners, as the priest, the nuns, and her lawyer stepped away.

The commander of the firing squad, who had been watching his men attentively to prevent them from examining their rifles—it is customary to always put a blank cartridge in one, so that everyone can claim not to have fired the deadly shot—seemed to relax. Soon the business would be over.

"Ready!"

The twelve men took a rigid stance and placed their rifles at their shoulders.

Mata Hari did not move a muscle.

The officer stood where all the soldiers could see him and raised his sword.

"Aim!"

The woman before them remained impassive, showing no fear.

The officer's sword dropped, slicing through the air in an arc.

"Fire!"

The sun, now rising on the horizon, illuminated the flames and small puffs of smoke issuing from the rifles as a flurry of gunfire rang out with a bang. Immediately after this, the soldiers returned their rifles to the ground in a rhythmic motion.

For a fraction of a second, Mata Hari remained upright. She did not die the way you see in moving pictures after people are shot. She did not plunge forward or backward, and she did not throw her arms up or to the side. She collapsed onto herself, her head still up, her eyes still open. One of the soldiers fainted.

Then her knees buckled and her body fell to the right, legs doubled up beneath the fur coat. And there she lay, motionless, with her face turned toward the heavens.

A third officer drew his revolver from a holster strapped to his chest and, accompanied by a lieutenant, walked toward the motionless body.

Bending over, he placed the muzzle of the revolver against the spy's temple, taking care not to touch her skin. Then he pulled the trigger, and the bullet tore through her brain. He turned to all who were present and said in a solemn voice:

"Mata Hari is dead."

Part I

Dear Mr. Clunet,

I do not know what will happen at the end of this week. I have always been an optimistic woman, but time has left me bitter, alone, and sad.

If things turn out as I hope, you will never receive this letter. I'll have been pardoned. After all, I spent my life cultivating influential friends. I will hold on to the letter so that, one day, my only daughter might read it to find out who her mother was.

But if I am wrong, I have little hope that these pages, which have consumed my last week of life on Earth, will be kept. I have always been a realistic woman and I know that, once a case is settled, a lawyer will move on to the next one without a backward glance.

I can imagine what will happen after. You will be a very busy man, having gained notoriety defending a war criminal. You will have many people knocking at your door, begging for your services, for, even defeated, you attracted huge publicity. You will meet journalists interested to hear your version of events, you will dine in the city's most expensive restaurants, and you will be looked upon with respect and envy by your peers. You will know there was never any concrete evidence against me—only documents that had been tampered with—but you will never publicly admit that you allowed an innocent woman to die.

Innocent? Perhaps that is not the right word. I was never innocent, not since I first set foot in this city I love so dearly. I thought I could manipulate those who wanted state secrets. I thought the Germans, French, English, Spanish would never be able to resist me—and yet, in the end, I was the one manipulated. The crimes I did commit, I escaped, the greatest of which was being an emancipated and independent woman in a world ruled by men. I was convicted of espionage even though the only thing concrete I traded was the gossip from high-society salons.

Yes, I turned this gossip into "secrets," because I wanted money and power. But all those who accuse me now know I never revealed anything new.

It's a shame no one will know this. These envelopes will inevitably find their way to a dusty file cabinet, full of documents from other proceedings. Perhaps they will leave when your successor, or your successor's successor, decides to make room and throw out old cases.

By that time, my name will have been long forgotten. But I am not writing to be remembered. I am attempting to understand things myself. Why? How is it that a woman who for so many years got everything she wanted can be condemned to death for so little?

At this moment, I look back at my life and realize that memory is a river, one that always runs backward.

Memories are full of caprice, where images of things we've experienced are still capable of suffocating us through one small detail or insignificant sound. The smell of baking bread wafts up to my cell and reminds me of the days I walked freely in the cafés. This tears me apart more than my fear of death or the solitude in which I now find myself.

Memories bring with them a devil called melancholy—oh, cruel demon that I cannot escape. Hearing a prisoner singing, receiving a small handful of letters from admirers who were never among those who brought me roses and jasmine flowers, picturing a scene from some city I didn't appreciate at the time. Now it's all I have left of this or that country I visited.

The memories always win, and with them comes a demon that is even more terrifying than melancholy: remorse. It's my only companion in this cell, except when the sisters decide to come and chat. They do not speak about God, or condemn me for what society calls my "sins of the flesh." Generally, they say one or two words, and the memories spout from my mouth, as if I wanted to go back in time, plunging into this river that runs backward.

One of them asked me:

"If God gave you a second chance, would you do anything differently?"

I said yes, but really, I do not know. All I know is that my current heart is a ghost town, one populated by passions, enthusiasm, loneliness, shame, pride, betrayal, and sadness. I cannot disentangle myself from any of it, even when I feel sorry for myself and weep in silence.

I am a woman who was born at the wrong time and nothing can be done to fix this. I don't know if the future will remember me, but if it does, may it never see me as a victim, but as someone who moved forward with courage, fearlessly paying the price she had to pay.

On one of my trips to Vienna I met a gentleman who had become a roaring success in Austria among men and women alike. He was called Freud—I can't remember his first name—and people adored him because he had restored the possibility that we are all innocent. Our faults were actually those of our parents.

I try to see now where mine went wrong, but I cannot blame my family. Adam and Antje Zelle gave me everything money could buy. They owned a hat shop and invested in oil before people knew of its importance, which allowed me to attend a private school, study dance, take riding lessons. When people started to accuse me of being a "woman of easy

virtue," my father wrote a book in my defense—
something he should have never done. I was perfectly at ease with what I was doing, and his words
only drew more attention to their accusations of
prostitution and lying.

Yes, I was a prostitute—if by that you mean someone who receives favors and jewelry in exchange for
affection and pleasure. Yes, I was a liar, one so com-
pulsive and out of control that I often forgot what
I'd said and had to expend great mental energy to
cover my blunders.

I cannot blame my parents for anything, except
perhaps for having given birth to me in the wrong
town. Leeuwarden, a place most of my fellow Dutch-
men will have never even heard of, is a town where
absolutely nothing happens and every day is the
same as the last. Early on, as a teenager, I learned
that I was beautiful from the way my friends used
to imitate me.

In 1889, my family's fortune changed—Adam
went bankrupt and Antje fell ill, dying two years
later. They did not want me to have to go through
what they went through, and sent me away to school
in another city, Leiden, firm in their objective that I

have the finest education. There I trained to become a kindergarten teacher while I awaited the arrival of a husband who would take charge of me. On the day of my departure, my mother called me over and gave me a packet of seeds:

"Take this with you, Margaretha."

Margaretha—Margaretha Zelle—was my name, and I detested it. Countless girls had been given the name Margaretha because of a famous and well-respected actress.

I asked what the seeds were for.

"They're tulip seeds, the symbol of our country. But, more than that, they represent a truth you must learn. These seeds will always be tulips, even if at the moment you cannot tell them apart from other flowers. They will never turn into roses or sunflowers, no matter how much they might desire to. And if they try to deny their own existence, they will live life bitter and die.

"So you must learn to follow your destiny, whatever it may be, with joy. As flowers grow, they show off their beauty and are appreciated by all; then, after they die, they leave their seeds so that others may continue God's work."

She placed the packet of seeds in a small bag that I had watched her stitch carefully for days despite her illness.

"Flowers teach us that nothing is permanent: not their beauty, not even the fact that they will inevitably wilt, because they will still give new seeds. Remember this when you feel joy, pain, or sadness. Everything passes, grows old, dies, and is reborn."

How many storms must I weather before I understand this? At the time, her words sounded hollow; I was eager to leave that suffocating town, with its identical days and nights. And yet today, as I write this, I understand that my mother was also talking about herself.

"Even the tallest trees are able to grow from tiny seeds like these. Remember this, and try not to rush time."

She gave me a kiss goodbye, and my father took me to the train station. We barely spoke on our way there.

All the men I've known have given me joy, jewelry, or a place in society, and I've never regretted knowing them—all except the first, the school principal, who raped me when I was sixteen.

He called me into his office, locked the door, then placed his hand between my legs and began to masturbate. At first I tried to escape, saying, gently, that this wasn't the time or place. But he said nothing. He pushed aside some papers on his desk, laid me on my stomach, and penetrated me all in one go, as if he were scared that someone might enter the room and see us.

My mother had taught me, in a conversation laden with metaphors, that "intimacy" with a man should take place only when there is love, and when that love is for life. I left his office confused and frightened, determined not to tell anyone what had happened, until another girl brought it up when we were talking in a group. From what I could tell, it had already happened to two of them, but to whom could we complain? We risked being expelled from school and sent back home, unable to explain the reason. So we were forced to keep quiet. My solace was knowing I wasn't the only one. Later, when I became famous in Paris for my dance performances, these girls told others and, before long, all of Leiden knew what had happened. The principal had already retired, and no one dared confront him. Quite the opposite! Some even envied him for having been the beau of the great diva of the time.

From that experience, I began to associate sex with something mechanical, something that had nothing to do with love.

Leiden was even worse than Leeuwarden; there was the famous training school for kindergarten teachers, and a bunch of people who had nothing better to do than mind other people's business. One day, out of boredom, I began reading the classified ads in the newspaper of a neighboring town. And there it was: *Rudolf MacLeod, an officer in the Dutch army of Scottish descent, currently stationed in Indonesia, seeks young bride to get married and live abroad.*

There was my salvation! Officer. Indonesia. Strange seas and exotic worlds. Enough of conservative, Calvinist Holland, full of prejudice and boredom. I answered the ad, enclosing the best and most sensual picture I had. Little did I know that the ad had been placed as a joke by one of the captain's friends. My letter would be the last of sixteen to arrive.

He came to meet me dressed as if he were going to war: in full uniform, with a sword hanging to the left, and his long whiskers coated in pomade, which somewhat hid his ugliness and lack of manners.

At our first meeting, we talked about trivial matters. I prayed for him to return, and my prayers were answered; a week later he was back, to the envy of my girlfriends and the despair of the school principal, who possibly still dreamed of another day like the one before. I noticed Rudolf smelled like alcohol, but did not pay it much mind. He was likely nervous in my presence, me a young woman who, according to all my friends, was the most beautiful in the class.

He asked me to marry him on our third and final meeting. Indonesia. Army captain. Voyages to faraway places. What more could a young woman want from life?

"You're going to marry a man twenty-one years your senior? Does he know you're no longer a virgin?" asked one of the girls who had had the same experience with the school principal.

I didn't answer. I returned home, he respectfully asked my family for my hand, and they took a loan from the neighbors for the trousseau. We were married on July 11, 1895, three months after reading the ad.

"Change" and *"change for the better"* are two very different things. If it weren't for dance and for an officer named Andreas, my years in Indonesia would have been a never-ending nightmare. My worst nightmare now would be to go through it all again. A distant husband who was always surrounded by other women, the impossibility of running away and returning home, the loneliness that came from being forced to spend months indoors because I didn't speak the language, not to mention being constantly kept tabs on by the other officers.

What should have been a source of joy for any woman—the birth of her children—would become a nightmare for me. After I recovered from the pain of childbirth, my life was filled with meaning the first time I touched my daughter's tiny body. Rudolf improved his behavior for a few months, but soon he returned to what he liked best: his local lovers. According to him, no European woman could compete with an Asian woman, for whom sex was like a dance. He told me this without any shame, perhaps because he was drunk, or perhaps because he deliberately wanted to humiliate me. Later, Andreas shared that, one night when the two of them were on a meaningless expedition from nothingness to nowhere, Rudolf said in a moment of alcoholic candor:

"I'm afraid of Margaretha. Have you noticed how the other officers look at her? She could leave me at any moment."

It was this sick logic, one that turns men afraid of losing someone into monsters, that made him grow even worse. He called me a whore because I wasn't a virgin when I met him. He wanted to know the details of every man he imagined I'd once had. Sobbing, I told him the story of the principal in his office. Sometimes he'd beat me, saying I was lying, and other times he masturbated and demanded more details. Given that it had been a nightmare for me, I was forced to invent these, not quite understanding why I was doing it.

He went so far as to send a servant with me to buy something that looked like the school uniform I'd worn when he met me. Whenever he was possessed by some unknown demon, he'd order me to wear it. He took the most pleasure from reenacting the rape scene; he would lay me down on the desk and penetrate me violently as I cried out, so all the servants could hear and assume that I loved it.

Sometimes I had to behave like a good little girl, who endured the rape; other times he made me scream for him to be more violent, like I was a whore and liked it.

Gradually I lost sight of who I was. My days were spent caring for my daughter, shuffling about the house with a vacant look on my face. I concealed the scratches and bruises under extra makeup, but I knew I wasn't fooling anyone.

I fell pregnant again. I enjoyed a few days of immense happiness caring for my son, but he was soon poisoned by one of his nannies, who never even had the opportunity to explain her actions;

the other servants killed her the same day the baby was found dead. In the end, most said it was deserved retaliation, as the nanny had been constantly beaten, raped, and burdened by endless working hours.

Now I had only my daughter, a house that was always empty, a husband who never took me anywhere for fear of being betrayed, and a city so beautiful it felt oppressive; here I was in paradise, living my own personal hell.

Then one day, everything changed. The regiment commander invited the officers and their wives to a local dance performance meant to honor one of the island's rulers. Rudolf could never say no to a superior. He asked me to buy something expensive and sensual to wear. I understood the reason for "expensive," which spoke more to his possessions than my own personal endowments. But if—as I learned later—he was so afraid of me, why would he want me to dress sensually?

We arrived at the venue. The women looked at me with envy, the men with desire, and I noticed that that excited Rudolf. It looked like the evening would end badly, with me being forced to describe what I had "imagined doing" with each of the officers as Rudolf penetrated and beat me. By any means possible, I had to protect the only thing I had left: myself. And the only way I was able to do that was by striking up a long conversation with Andreas, whose wife watched me with terror and amazement. I kept my husband's glass full, hoping he would fall over drunk.

I would like to finish writing about Java here, this instant; when the past dredges up a memory capable of opening old wounds, suddenly other wounds appear and make the soul bleed more deeply, until you have to kneel down and cry. But I cannot stop until I bring up the three things that would change my life: my decision, the dance we watched, and Andreas.

My decision: I could no longer accumulate problems and live so far beyond the limits of human suffering.

As I thought about this, the group that was preparing to dance for the local ruler began to take the stage, nine people in total. Instead of the frenetic, joyful, and expressive rhythms I had seen on my few visits to the city's theaters, everything seemed to happen in slow motion. At first I was bored to death, but was then overtaken by a kind of religious trance, as the dancers let themselves get carried away by the music and assumed impossible poses. In one, their bodies bent forward and backward, forming an extremely painful S; they remained there until, suddenly, they'd snap out of their stillness like leopards ready to ambush.

They were all painted blue and dressed in sarongs, the typical local attire. Across their chests, they wore a silk ribbon meant to emphasize the men's muscles and cover the women's breasts. The women, in turn, wore handcrafted tiaras decorated with precious stones. Moments of tenderness alternated with imitations of battles, where the silk ribbons served as imaginary swords.

I grew increasingly entranced. For the first time I understood that Rudolf, Holland, my slain son, all of these things were part of a world that had died and was being reborn, like the seeds my mother had given me. I looked to the sky and saw the stars and the palm leaves. I was ready to let myself be swept away to another dimension and another space when Andreas's voice interrupted:

"Do you understand everything?"

I thought I must, because my heart had stopped bleeding and was now beholding beauty in its purest form. Men, however, always need to explain something, and he told me this kind of *ballet* came from an ancient Indian tradition that combined yoga and meditation. He failed to understand that dance is a poem, one where each movement represents a word.

With my mental yoga and my spontaneous meditation interrupted, I found myself obliged to engage in any kind of conversation so as not to appear impolite.

Andreas's wife was watching him. Andreas was watching me. Rudolf was watching me, Andreas, and one of the leader's female guests, who returned his courtesy with a smile.

We talked for a while, despite the dirty looks coming from the Javanese because none of the foreigners were respecting their sacred ritual. Perhaps that is why the show came to a close earlier than expected, with all the dancers filing out in a procession, eyes fixed on their fellow countrymen. None of them looked at the white barbarians with their well-dressed wives, their raucous laughter, their Vaseline-coated beards and mustaches, and their terrible manners.

After I filled his glass once more, Rudolf walked toward the Javanese woman who had smiled, and she looked at him without any fear or intimidation. Andreas's wife came over, grabbed his arm, smiled in a way that said "He's mine," and pretended to be most interested in her husband's pointless commentary about the dance.

"All these years I have been faithful to you," she said, suddenly interrupting the conversation.

"You are the one who commands my heart and my actions, and, God is my witness, every night I ask for you to return home safe and sound. If I had to give my life for yours, I would do it without any fear."

Turning to me, Andreas excused himself and said he had to leave, that the ceremony had been very tiring for everyone. But his wife said she would not budge; she said it with such authority that her husband did not dare make another move.

"I waited patiently for you to understand that you are the most important thing in my life. I followed you to this place. While beautiful, it must be a nightmare for all the wives, including Margaretha."

She turned to me then, her big blue eyes pleading for my agreement, for me to follow in that ancient tradition women had of always being one another's enemy and accomplice. But I didn't have the courage to nod.

"I fought for our love with all my might, but today it's run out. The stone that weighed on my heart is now a rock that will no longer let it beat. And my heart, with its last breath, told me there are other worlds beyond this one, worlds where I don't have to always beg for the company of a man to fill these empty days and nights."

Something told me that tragedy was coming. I asked her to calm down; she was very dear to everyone in that group, and her husband was a model officer. She shook her head and smiled, as if she'd already heard it many times. And she continued:

"My body can keep breathing, but my soul is dead. I cannot leave here, nor can I make you understand I need you by my side."

Andreas, an officer of the Dutch army with a

reputation to preserve, was visibly uncomfortable. I turned and began to walk away, but she dropped her husband's arm and held on to mine.

"Only love can give meaning to something that, on its own, has none at all. It turns out I don't have that love. So what reason is there to go on living?"

Her face was right next to mine; I tried to smell for alcohol on her breath, but there was none. I looked in her eyes and also saw no tears. Perhaps they had all dried.

"Please, I need you to stay, Margaretha. You are a good woman, one who lost a child. Though I've never been pregnant, I know what that means. I'm not doing this for me, but for all those women who are prisoners in their alleged freedom."

Before any of us had time to stop her, Andreas's wife slid a small pistol from her purse, pointed it to her own heart, and fired. Though much of the noise had been absorbed by her evening gown, people turned our way. At first they must have thought I had committed the crime, as, seconds earlier, she was clinging to me. But soon they saw the look of horror on my face and Andreas kneeling, trying to stanch the blood carrying away his wife's life. She died in his arms, her eyes displaying nothing but peace. Everyone drew near, including Rudolf, the Javanese woman having taken off in the opposite direction, afraid of what might happen with so many armed and drunken men. Before people began to ask what had happened, I asked my husband if we could leave right away; he agreed without saying a word.

When we got home, I went straight to my bedroom and began to pack my clothes. Rudolf fell onto the sofa, completely drunk. The next morning, after he awoke and ate a hearty breakfast served by the staff, he came to my room and saw the suitcases. It was the first time he broached the subject.

"Where do you think you're going?"

"To Holland, on the next ship. Either that or heaven, as soon as I get the same opportunity that Andreas's wife had. You decide."

He was the only one used to giving orders. But the look in my eyes must have changed, because, after a moment's hesitation, he left the house. When he returned that night, he said we really did need to make use of the leave to which he was entitled. Two weeks later we set off on the first ship to Rotterdam.

I had been baptized with the blood of Andreas's wife and, through that rite, I was freed forever, though neither of us knew how far this freedom would reach.

Part of what precious time I have left—though I still have great hopes of being pardoned by the president, as I have many friends among the ministers— was taken today by Sister Laurence, who brought me a list of items that were in my luggage when I was arrested.

With all the care in the world, she asked what she should do with it, should the worst-case scenario present itself. I asked her to leave me alone, and said that I would return to it later, because at the moment I have no time to waste. But if the worst scenario does indeed become the only one, she can do whatever she wants. In any event, I am copying everything down here, for I believe that everything will turn out for the best.

Trunk 1

1 gold watch adorned with blue lacquer and
bought in Switzerland; and

1 round box containing 6 hats, 3 pins in pearl
and gold, some long feathers, a veil, 2 fur
stoles, 3 adornments for a hat, a pear-shaped
brooch, and a ball gown.

Trunk 2

1 pair of riding boots;

1 horse brush;

1 box of shoe polish;

1 pair of spats;

1 pair of spurs;

5 pairs of leather shoes;

3 white shirts to match riding clothes;

1 napkin—I don't know what it is doing taking
up space there; perhaps I used it to polish
my boots;

1 pair of leather gaiters, protection for the legs;

3 sets of special breast supporters, so they look
firm during a gallop;

8 pairs of silk underpants and 2 cotton;

2 belts to match with different riding clothes;

4 pairs of gloves;

1 umbrella;

3 visors to avoid direct sun in the eyes;

3 pairs of wool socks, though one of them is
    already worn from use;

1 special bag for storing dresses;

15 sanitary towels for menstruation;

1 wool sweater;

1 full riding costume, with matching jacket
    and trousers;

1 box with hair barrettes;

1 lock of fake hair extension, with a clip to
    attach it to my natural hair;

3 fox-fur neck-warmers; and

2 boxes of face powder.

Trunk 3

6 pairs of garters;

1 box of skin moisturizer;

3 pairs of patent-leather high-heel boots;

2 corsets;

34 dresses;

1 handmade cloth bag, with what appears
    to be seeds of unidentified plants;

8 bodices;

1 shawl;

10 pairs of more comfortable underpants;

3 waistcoats;

2 long-sleeved jackets;

3 combs;

16 blouses;

Another ball gown;

1 towel and 1 bar of scented soap—
  I do not use hotel soaps, as they can transmit
  diseases;

1 pearl necklace;

1 handbag with mirror inside;

1 ivory comb;

2 boxes for putting away my jewelry before
  sleeping;

1 copper case with calling cards, in the name of
  Vadime de Massloff, Capitaine du première
  Régiment Spécial Impérial Russe;

1 wooden box containing a porcelain tea service
  I was given during the trip;

2 nightgowns;

1 nail file with mother-of-pearl handle;

2 cigarette cases, 1 in silver and 1 in gold,
  or gold-plated, I'm not sure;

8 hairnets for bedtime;

Boxes with necklaces, earrings, an emerald ring,
another ring with emeralds and diamonds,
and other costume jewelry of little value;

Silk bag with 21 scarves and handkerchiefs
inside;

3 fans;

Lipstick and rouge from the best brand France
can produce;

1 French dictionary;

1 wallet with several photos of me; and . . .

A great deal of nonsense I intend to get rid of
once I am released from here, such as letters
from lovers tied with special silk ribbons,
used tickets from operas I enjoyed watching,
things like that.

Most of this was confiscated by the Hôtel Meurice in Paris, because they thought—wrongly, of course—that I wouldn't have the money to pay for my stay. How could they think that? After all, Paris was always my preferred destination; I would never leave them to think of me as a swindler.

I was not asking to be happy; I was asking only to not be as unhappy and miserable as I felt. Perhaps, if I'd had a bit more patience, I would have left for Paris under different circumstances. But I could no longer stand the recrimination of my father's new wife, my husband, a child who cried all the time, or the small town filled with provincial people still prejudiced against me even though now I was a married and respectable woman.

One day, I took a train to The Hague and went to the French consulate without anyone knowing— something that demands great intuition and skill. The drums of war were not yet beating, and entering the country was still easy; Holland had always remained neutral in the conflicts that ravaged

Europe, and I had confidence. I met with the consul, and after two hours in a café, during which he attempted to seduce me and I pretended to fall into his trap, I got a one-way ticket to Paris. I promised to wait for him there until he could escape for a few days.

"I know how to be generous with those who help me," I hinted. He got the message and asked what I could do.

"I'm a classical dancer to oriental music."

Oriental music? That piqued his curiosity even more. I asked if he could get me a job. He said he could introduce me to a very powerful man in the city, Monsieur Guimet, who, in addition to being a great art collector, loved everything from the East. When was I ready to depart?

"This very day, if you can arrange a place for me to stay."

He realized he was being manipulated. I was just another one of those women who venture to the city of dreams in pursuit of wealthy men and an easy life. I sensed he was starting to pussyfoot. He was listening but, at the same time, observing my every move, word, and gesture. Contrary to what you might think, I—who had been behaving like a

femme fatale—was now acting like the most mod-
est person in the world.

"If your friend likes, I can show him one or two
authentic Javanese dances. If he doesn't like them,
I'll be back on the train that same day."

"But, Madam . . ."

"Miss."

"You asked for only a one-way ticket."

I took some money from my pocket and showed
him I had enough to return. I also had enough to
go, but letting a man help a woman leaves him vulnerable. This is the dream of all men, according to
the officers' mistresses in Java.

He relaxed and asked my name so he could write
a letter of referral to Monsieur Guimet. I had never
thought of that! A name? My real name would lead
to my family, and the last thing France wanted was
to create a situation with a neutral nation because
of a woman who was desperate to escape.

"Your name?" he repeated, pen and paper in
hand.

"Mata Hari."

The blood of Andreas's wife was baptizing me
again.

I couldn't believe what I was seeing. A giant iron tower stretched to the heavens, yet wasn't on any of the city's postcards. Lining both banks of the Seine were distinctive buildings in the style of China, Italy, and other of the world's most illustrious countries. I tried to find Holland, but could not. What represented my country? The old windmills? Heavy wooden shoes? Neither of those had a place among all these modern things—marvels I couldn't believe existed were announced on the posters mounted on circular iron bases.

"Look! Lights that turn on and off without needing to use gas or fire! Only at the Palace of Electricity!"

"Go up the stairs without moving your feet! The

steps do it for you." This one was under a drawing of a structure that looked like an open tunnel, with handrails on both sides.

"Art Nouveau: fashion's latest trend."

There was no exclamation point on that one, just a photograph of a vase with two porcelain swans. Below it was a drawing of what looked to be a metal structure similar to the giant tower, with the pompous name *Grand Palais*.

Cinéorama, Mareorama, Panorama—all promised moving images that could transport visitors to places where they'd never before dreamed of going. The more I looked, the more lost I got. And also the more full of regret; I might have taken a bigger step than my legs could stretch.

The city teemed with people, walking from one end of the banks to the other. Women dressed with an elegance I'd never seen in my life, and the men seemed busy with important matters, but whenever I turned back, I noticed their eyes were following me.

Though French was taught in school, I was very insecure. With a dictionary in hand, I approached a young woman who must have been more or less my age and asked, with great difficulty, how to find the hotel the consul had reserved for me. She looked at my luggage and clothes and, though I was wearing the best dress I'd brought back from Java, continued on her way without answering. Apparently foreigners were not welcome, or Parisians thought they were superior to all other peoples of the earth.

I repeated my attempt two or three times, and the reply was always the same, until I grew tired and sat down on a bench in the Jardin des Tuileries. This was a dream I'd had since childhood; just making it here was almost achievement enough.

Should I turn back? I debated with myself for a while, knowing how difficult it would be to find the place to sleep. Then fate intervened: A strong wind blew, and a top hat came knocking right between my legs.

Picking it up carefully, I stood to hand it to the man running to meet me.

"I see you have my hat," he said.

"Yes, your hat was drawn to my legs," I replied.

"I can see why," he said, not disguising a clear attempt to seduce me. Unlike the Calvinists of my country, the French had a reputation for being completely and utterly liberated.

He reached out to take the hat, but I put it behind

my back and extended my other hand, where the hotel address was written. After reading, he asked me what it was.

"A friend of mine lives there. I came to spend two days with her."

I couldn't say I was on my way to have dinner with her, because he saw the luggage beside me.

He said nothing. I figured the place must be so low as to be not worth criticizing, but his reply was a surprise:

"Rue de Rivoli is just behind this bench where you are seated. I can carry your suitcase, and there are several bars along the way. Would you have an anise liqueur with me, Madame . . ."

"Mademoiselle Mata Hari."

I had nothing to lose. He was to be my first friend in the city. We walked toward the hotel and, on the way, we stopped at a restaurant where the waiters wore long aprons down to their feet and dressed as though they had just left a formal gala. They smiled for practically no one, except for my companion, whose name I've forgotten. We found a table tucked away in a corner of the restaurant.

He asked me where I came from. "The East

Indies," I explained. "Part of the Dutch empire, and where I was born and raised." I commented on the beautiful tower, perhaps the only one like it in the world, and unwittingly awakened his wrath.

"It will be dismantled four years from now. This World's Fair has cost the government coffers more than our two most recent wars. They want us to think that, from now on, we'll have a union of all the countries of Europe and finally live in peace. Can you believe that?"

I had no opinion, so I preferred to keep quiet. As I said before, men love to explain things, and they have opinions on everything.

"You should have seen the pavilion the Germans built. They tried to humiliate us. It was this huge thing, in poor taste, full of installations with machinery, metallurgy, miniature ships said to soon dominate all the seas, and a giant tower filled with . . ."

He paused as if preparing to say something obscene.

". . . beer! They say it's in honor of the kaiser, but I am absolutely certain the entire collection serves only one purpose: to warn us to be careful. Ten years ago they arrested a Jewish spy who guaranteed war would be knocking at our doors again. But nowadays they swear the poor guy is innocent, and all because of that damn writer, Zola. He's managed to divide our society. Now half of France wants to free him from Devil's Island, where he should stay forever."

He ordered two more glasses of anise, drank his with haste, and then said he was very busy, but, should I be staying in town longer, I ought to visit my country's pavilion.

My country? I hadn't seen any windmills or wooden shoes.

"Actually, they gave it the wrong name: It's the Pavilion of the East Indies of Holland. I haven't had time to go—I'm sure it's there for the same reason as all the other overly expensive installations—but I've heard it is very interesting."

He got up. Taking out a calling card, he pulled a gold pen from his pocket and crossed out his second name, a sign that he hoped we might one day become closer.

He left, bidding farewell with a formal kiss on the hand. I looked at the card. According to tradition, it had no address. I wasn't about to start accumulating useless things, so as soon as he was out of sight, I crumpled it and threw it away.

Two minutes later I went back to get the card; that was the man to whom the consul's letter was addressed!

Part II

Slender and tall, with the lithe grace of a wild animal, Mata Hari has black hair that undulates strangely and transports us to a magical place.

The most feminine of all women, writing an unfamiliar tragedy with her body.

A thousand curves and movements combine perfectly with a thousand different rhythms.

The lines from these newspaper clippings seem like pieces of a broken teacup, telling the story of a life I no longer remember. As soon as I get out of here, I will have the clippings bound in leather, each page with a gold frame. They shall be my bequest to my daughter, as all my money was confiscated. When we are reunited, I will tell her about the Folies Bergère, the dream of every woman who has ever wished to dance before an audience. I will tell her how beautiful Madrid de los Austrias is, as are the streets of Berlin, the palaces in Monte Carlo. We will tour the Trocadéro and the Cercle Royal, and we will go to Maxim's, Rumpelmeyer's, and all the other restaurants that will rejoice at the return of their most famous customer.

Together, we will go to Italy and delight to see that damned Diaghilev on the verge of bankruptcy. I will show her La Scala in Milan and say proudly:

"Here is where I danced *Bacchus and Gambrinus* by Marceno."

I am sure that what I am going through now will only add to my reputation; who wouldn't want to be seen as a femme fatale, an alleged "spy" full of secrets? Everyone flirts with danger, so long as that danger does not really exist.

Perhaps she will ask me:

"And what about my mother, Margaretha MacLeod?"

And I will reply:

"I do not know who that woman is. All my life I've thought and acted like Mata Hari, the woman who has been and always will be the fascination of men and the envy of women. Ever since I left Holland, I've lost all sense of distance and danger—neither scares me. I arrived in Paris with no money and no proper wardrobe, and just look at how I've moved up. I hope the same happens to you."

And I will talk about my dances—thankfully, I have pictures showing most of the movements and costumes. Contrary to what the critics who never understood me said, when I was onstage I simply forgot about the woman I was and offered everything to God. That is why I was able to undress so easily. At that moment, I was nothing, not even my body. I was just movements communing with the universe.

I will always be grateful to Monsieur Guimet. He gave me my first chance to perform, at his private museum, and in very expensive clothes he had imported from Asia for his personal collection, although it did cost me half an hour of sex and very little pleasure. I danced for an audience of three hundred people, including journalists, celebrities, and at least two ambassadors—one from Japan and one from Germany. Two days later, it was all the papers could talk about, this exotic woman who had been born in a remote corner of the Dutch empire and brought the "religiousness" and "disin-hibition" of people from distant lands.

The museum stage had been decorated with a statue of Shiva—the Hindu god of creation and destruction. Candles burned in aromatic oils and the music left everyone in a kind of trance, except me—after having carefully examined the clothes I'd been entrusted, I knew exactly what I planned to do. It was now or never, a single moment in my heretofore miserable life, one where I was always asking for favors in exchange for sex. I was used to it by then, but it is one thing to get used to something, another to be satisfied. Money was not enough. I wanted more!

When I started dancing, I knew I needed to do something that only the dancers in cabarets did, without bothering to give any meaning to it. I was in a respectable place, with an audience who was eager for new things but lacked the courage to visit the certain kinds of places where they might be seen.

The clothing was formed of veils layered one on top of the other. I removed the first one and no one seemed to pay much notice. But when I removed the second, then the third, people began to exchange glances. By the fifth veil, the audience was totally focused on what I was doing, caring little about the dance but wondering how far I would go. Even the women, whose eyes I met now and then between movements, did not seem shocked or angry; it must have excited them as much as it did the men. I knew that were I in my country, I would be sent to prison immediately, but France was an example of equality and freedom.

When I got to the sixth veil, I went over to the Shiva statue, simulated an orgasm, and cast myself to the ground while removing the seventh and final veil.

For a few moments I did not hear a single sound from the audience—from where I was lying, I could not see anyone, and they seemed petrified or horrified. Then came the first "Bravo," spoken by a

female voice, and soon the whole room rose for a
standing ovation. I got up with one arm covering
my breasts and the other extended to cover my sex.
I bowed my head in appreciation and walked off the
stage to where I had strategically left a silk robe. I
returned, continued to give thanks for the unceas-
ing applause, and decided it was better to leave and
not come back. This was part of the mystery.

I noticed, however, that one person did not
applaud, only smiled. Madame Guimet.

Two invitations arrived the next morning. One was from a Madame Kireyevsky, asking if I might repeat the same dance performance at a charity ball to raise funds for wounded Russian soldiers, and the other from Madame Guimet, who invited me for a walk along the banks of the Seine.

The newsstands were not yet plastered in post-cards of my face, and there were no cigarettes, cigars, or bath lotions with my name. I was still an illustrious unknown, but I had made the most important step; each member of the audience had left enthralled, and this would be the best publicity I could ask for.

"It's a good thing that people are ignorant," Madame Guimet said, "because nothing you performed belongs to any Eastern tradition. You must have hatched each step as the evening wore on."

I froze, and wondered if her next comment would be about the fact I had spent the night—one simple, single, unpleasant night—with her husband.

"The only ones who would know that, however, are those deathly boring anthropologists who learn everything from books; they'll never be able to give you away."

"But I . . ."

"Yes, I believe you went to Java and you know the local customs, and perhaps you were the lover or wife of some officer in your army. Like all young women, you dreamed of one day making it big in Paris; that's why you ran away at the first opportunity and came here."

We kept walking, now in silence. I could go on lying—I'd done it my entire life, and I could lie about anything, except for what Madame Guimet already knew. Better to wait and see where this conversation was going.

"I have some advice for you," said Madame Guimet, when we started across the bridge that led to the gigantic metal tower.

I asked if we could sit. It was difficult for me to concentrate as we walked among the crowds of people. She agreed, and we found a bench on the Champ de Mars. Some men, serious and pensive, tossed metal balls and tried to hit a piece of wood; the scene was ludicrous to me.

"I spoke with some friends who attended your performance, and I know that tomorrow the newspapers will have you up on a pedestal. But don't worry about me; I won't say a word to anyone about your 'oriental dance.'"

I continued listening. I couldn't argue about anything.

"My first piece of advice is the hardest, and it has nothing to do with your performance. Never fall in love. Love is a poison. Once you fall in love, you lose control over your life—your heart and mind belong to someone else. Your existence is threatened. You start to do everything to hold on to your loved one and lose all sense of danger. Love, that inexplicable and dangerous thing, sweeps everything you are from the face of the earth and, in its place, leaves only what your beloved wants you to be."

I remembered the look in the eyes of Andreas's wife before she shot herself. Love kills suddenly, leaving no evidence of the crime.

A boy went up to a pushcart to buy ice cream. Madame Guimet used that to launch into her second piece of advice.

"People say life is not that complicated, but life is very complicated. What's simple is wanting an ice cream, a doll, or to win a game of *pétanque* like those men over there—fathers, with responsibilities, sweating and suffering as they try to get a stupid metal ball to hit a little piece of wood. Simple is wanting to be famous, but staying that way for more than a month or a year, especially when that fame is linked to one's body, is what is hard. Simple is wanting a man with all your heart, but that becomes impossible and complicated when that man is married with children and wouldn't leave his family for anything in this world."

She took a long pause. Her eyes filled with tears, and I realized she was speaking from experience.

It was my turn to talk. In a single breath I told her that yes, I had lied; I wasn't born, nor had I been raised, in the Dutch East Indies, but I knew the place well, not to mention the suffering of the women who went there in search of independence and excitement but found only loneliness and boredom. As faithfully as possible, I tried to reproduce Andreas's wife's final conversation with her husband, seeking to comfort Madame Guimet without revealing I knew she was talking about herself in all the advice she gave me.

"Everything in this world has two sides. People who were abandoned by the cruel god called love are also culpable, because they look into the past and wonder why they made so many plans for the future. But if they searched their memories even more, they would remember the day the seed was planted, and how they tended it, fertilized it, and let it grow until it became a tree that could never be uprooted."

Instinctively, my hand went to the place in my bag where I kept the seeds my mother gave me before she died. I always carried them with me.

"When a woman or a man is abandoned by the person they love, they are focused on their own pain. No one stops to wonder what is happening to the other person. Might they also be suffering, having left behind their own heart to stay with their families because of society? Every night they must lie in their beds, unable to sleep, confused and lost, wondering if they made the wrong decision. Other times, they feel certain it was their duty to protect their families and children. But time is not on their side; the more the moment of separation grows distant, the more their memories are purified of the difficult moments and turn into a longing for that paradise lost.

"The other person can no longer help himself. He becomes distant, he seems distracted during the week, and on Saturdays and Sundays he comes to the Champ de Mars to play ball with his friends. His son enjoys an ice cream, and his wife watches as the elegant dresses parade before her, a sad look in her eye. There's no wind strong enough to make the boat change direction; it stays in the harbor, venturing only among still waters. Everyone suffers; those who leave, those who stay, and their families and children. But no one can do anything."

Madame Guimet kept her eyes fixed on the newly planted grass at the center of the garden. She pretended she was just "tolerating" my words, but I knew I had opened an old wound that would begin to bleed again. After some time, she stood up and suggested we go back—her servants were likely already preparing dinner. An artist of growing fame and importance wanted to visit her husband's museum with his friends, and the evening would end with a visit to the artist's gallery, where he intended to show her some paintings.

"Of course, his intention is to try to sell me something, whereas my intention is to meet new and different people, to get outside a world that is beginning to bore me."

We strolled leisurely. Before crossing the bridge near the Trocadéro again, she asked me if I'd like to join them. I said yes, but that I'd left my evening gown at the hotel and might not be dressed appropriately for the occasion.

In truth, I did not have an evening gown that even came close to the elegance and beauty of the dresses we'd seen women wearing for a "stroll in the park." And the "hotel" was just a figure of speech for the boardinghouse I'd been living at for two months, the only one that allowed me to take "guests" to my bedroom.

But women are able to understand one another without exchanging a word.

"I can lend you a dress for tonight, if you like. I have more than I can ever wear."

I accepted her offer with a smile, and we headed back to her house.

When we don't know where life is taking us, we are never lost.

"*This is Pablo Picasso,* the artist I was telling you about."

From the moment we were introduced, Picasso forgot about the rest of the guests and spent the entire evening trying to strike up a conversation with me. He spoke of my beauty, asked me to pose for him, and said I needed to go with him to Málaga, if only to get a week away from the madness of Paris. He had one objective, and he didn't need to tell me what it was: to get me into his bed.

I was extremely embarrassed by that ugly, wide-eyed, impolite man who fancied himself the greatest of the greats. His friends were much more interesting, including an Italian man, Amedeo Modigliani, who seemed more noble, more elegant, and who at no point tried to force any conversation. Every time Pablo finished one of his interminable and incomprehensible lectures about the revolutions taking place in art, I turned to Modigliani. This seemed to infuriate Picasso.

"What do you do?" asked Amedeo.

I explained that I was devoted to the sacred dances of the tribes of Java. While he seemed to not quite understand, he politely began to talk about the importance of the eyes in dance. He was fascinated by eyes, and when he happened to go to the theater, he paid little attention to the movements of the bodies and instead concentrated on what the eyes were trying to say.

"I hope that happens in the sacred dances of Java—I know nothing about them. I know only that, in the East, they are able to keep their bodies completely still and concentrate the full force of what they want to say in the eyes."

As I did not know the answer, I merely bobbed my head, an enigmatic gesture that might mean yes or no depending on how he interpreted it. Picasso interrupted the conversation the whole time with his theories, but Amedeo, elegant and polite, knew to wait his turn and return to the subject.

"Can I give you some advice?" he asked, when the dinner was drawing to a close and everyone was preparing to go to Picasso's studio. I nodded yes.

"Know what you want and try to go beyond your own expectations. Improve your dancing, practice a lot, and set a very high goal, one that will be difficult to achieve. Because that is an artist's mission: to go beyond one's limits. An artist who desires very little and achieves it has failed in life."

The Spaniard's studio was not far away, so we all went on foot. Some things dazzled me, and others I simply detested. But isn't that the human condition? Going from one extreme to another, without stopping in the middle? To tease him, I stopped in front of one painting and asked why he insisted on complicating things.

"It took me four years to learn how to paint like a Renaissance master and my entire life to go back to drawing like a child. There's the real secret: children's drawings. What you're seeing may seem childish, but it represents what's most important in art."

His answer was brilliant, but I could no longer go back in time and change my mind about him. By then, Modigliani had already left, Madame Guimet was showing visible signs of exhaustion despite maintaining her composure, and Picasso was distracted by his girlfriend Fernande's jealousy.

I said it was getting late for all of us, and each went on his way. I never ran into Pablo or Amedeo again. I heard that Fernande decided to leave Pablo, but I was not told the exact reason. I saw her only once more, a few years later, when she was working as a clerk in an antiques shop. She did not recognize me, I pretended I did not recognize her, and she also disappeared from my life.

The years that followed weren't many, but when I think back today, they seem endless—I looked only toward the sunshine and forgot the storms. I let myself be dazzled by the beauty of the roses but paid no attention to the thorns. The lawyer who halfheartedly defended me in court was one of my many lovers. So Mr. Edouard Clunet, should things go exactly as you planned and I end up before a firing squad, you may rip out this page from the notebook and throw it away. Unfortunately, I have no one else in whom to confide. We all know I won't be killed because of this stupid allegation of espionage, but because I decided to be who I always dreamed. And the price of a dream is always high.

Strip-tease had been around—and allowed by

law—since the end of last century, but it had always been considered a mere display of flesh. I transformed that grotesque spectacle into art. When they began to ban strip-tease, I was able to continue with my shows, which were still legal. They were far from the vulgarity of other women who undressed in public. Among those who attended my performances were composers like Puccini and Massenet, ambassadors like Von Klunt and Antonio Gouvea, and magnates like baron de Rothschild and Gaston Menier. As I write these words, it pains me to think that they are not doing anything to obtain my freedom. After all, isn't the wrongly accused Captain Dreyfus back from Devil's Island?

Many will say: But he was innocent! Yes, and so am I. There is zero concrete evidence against me, beyond what I myself encouraged in order to boost my own importance after I decided to stop dancing (despite being an excellent dancer). If I hadn't, I wouldn't have been represented by the most important agent of the time, Mr. Astruc, who represented the greatest celebrities of the time.

Astruc nearly arranged for me to dance with Nijinsky at La Scala. But the ballet dancer's agent—

and lover—regarded me as a difficult, temperamental, and intolerable person. With a smile on his face, he insisted that I present my art all on my own, without support from the Italian press or the theater's own directors. And with that, part of my soul died. I knew I was getting older and soon would no longer have the same flexibility and lightness. And serious newspapers, which had praised me so much in the beginning, were turning against me.

And my imitators? Posters sprang up on every corner saying things like "the successor to Mata Hari." All they did was shake their bodies grotesquely and take off their clothes without artfulness or inspiration.

I cannot complain about Astruc, although at this point the last thing he likely wants is to see his name associated with mine. He appeared a few days after the series of benefit shows for wounded Russian soldiers. I sincerely doubted that all the money, raised by selling tables for princely sums, would find its way to the Pacific battlefields where the czar's men were taking a beating from the Japanese. Still, they were my first performances after the Guimet Museum, and everyone was pleased with the result.

I was able to get more people interested in my work, Madame Kireyevsky filled her coffers and mine, the aristocrats felt as though they were contributing to a good cause, and everyone, absolutely everyone, had the opportunity to see a beautiful naked woman without the slightest twinge of shame.

Astruc helped me find a hotel worthy of my rising fame and negotiated contracts throughout Paris. He got me a show at the Olympia, the most important concert hall of the time. The son of a Belgian rabbi, Astruc bet everything he had on total unknowns, and today they are icons, such as Caruso and Rubinstein. He took me out to see the world at just the right moment. Thanks to him, I changed the way I conducted myself, I began to earn more money than I ever before imagined, I performed in the city's major concert halls, and I could finally indulge in a luxury I appreciated more than anything else in the world: fashion.

I don't know how much I spent, because Astruc told me it was in poor taste to ask the price.

"Pick out whatever you like and have it sent to your hotel—I'll take care of the rest."

Now, as I write this, I'm beginning to wonder: Did he keep part of the money?

But I cannot think like that. I cannot keep this bitterness in my heart, because if I do get out of here—and that is what I expect to happen, because it is simply impossible to be abandoned by everyone—I will have just turned forty-one and want to have the right to be happy. I gained a lot of weight and can hardly go back to dancing, but the world has so much more than that.

I prefer to think of Astruc as the man who dared risk his entire fortune to build a theater and open with *The Rite of Spring*. It was by an unknown Russian composer whose name I still cannot remember, and starred that idiot Nijinsky, who imitated the masturbation scene from my first performance in Paris.

I prefer to remember Astruc as the man who once invited me to take the train and go to Normandy, because the day before we had both spoken, with nostalgia, of going too long without seeing the sea. We had been working together almost five years.

We sat there on the beach, neither of us saying much until I took a page from the newspaper in my bag and handed it to him.

"The Decadent Mata Hari: Lots of Exhibitionism but Little Talent," read the title of the article.

"It was published today," I said.

As he read, I got up, walked to the water's edge, and picked up some stones.

"Contrary to what you might think, I'm sick and tired. I've gotten away from my dreams and I'm not the person I imagined I'd be—not by far."

"What do you mean?" asked Astruc, surprised. "I only represent the greatest artists, and you are one of them! One simple review from someone who has nothing better to write is enough to leave you so beside yourself?"

"No, but it's the first thing I've read about myself in a long time. I'm disappearing from the theaters and the press. People see me as nothing more than a whore who strips naked in public under an artistic pretense."

Astruc got up and walked over to me. He also picked up a few stones from the beach and threw one into the water, far from the surf.

"I don't represent prostitutes—that would end my career. It's true that I've had to explain to one or two of my clients why I had a Mata Hari poster in my office. And you know what I said? That what you do is a retelling of a Sumerian myth in which the goddess Inanna goes to the forbidden world. She must pass through seven gates; at each, there waits a guardian, and, to pay her passage, she removes an article of clothing. A great English writer, who was exiled to Paris and died alone and destitute, wrote a play that will one day become a classic. It tells the story of how Herod got the head of John the Baptist."

"Salome! Where is that play?"

My spirits began to lift.

"I don't have the rights. And I can no longer meet with its author, Oscar Wilde, unless I go to the cemetery to summon his ghost. It's too late."

Again my frustration and misery returned, as did the idea that soon I would be old, ugly, and poor. I was over thirty—a pivotal age. I took a stone and threw it harder than Astruc had.

"Go far away, stone, and carry my past with you. All my shame, all my guilt, and all the mistakes I've made."

Astruc threw his stone and explained that I had made no mistakes. I had exercised my power of choice. I didn't listen to him, and threw another.

"And this one is for the abuse suffered by my body

and soul since my first, terrible sexual experience. And now, when I lie with rich men, performing acts that leave me drowning in tears. All this for influence, money, gowns . . . things that are growing old. I am tormented by self-created nightmares."

"But aren't you happy?" asked an increasingly surprised Astruc. After all, we had decided to spend a pleasant afternoon on the beach.

With ever-increasing rage, I kept throwing stones, becoming more and more surprised at myself. Tomorrow no longer looked like tomorrow, and the present was no longer the present, just a pit I dug deeper with every step. People walked on either side of me, while children played, seagulls made odd movements in the sky, and the waves rolled in more calmly than I imagined.

"It's because I dream of being accepted and respected, though I don't owe anything to anyone. Why do I need that? I waste my time on worries, regrets, and darkness—a darkness that only enslaves me, chaining me to a rock where I'm served up as food for birds of prey, a rock that I can no longer leave."

I couldn't cry. The stones disappeared into the

water, sinking alongside one another as if they could perhaps reconstruct Margaretha Zelle beneath the surface. But I did not want to be her again, that woman who looked into the eyes of Andreas's wife and understood. The one who told me that our lives are planned out down to the minutest details: You are born, go to school, and attend university in search of a husband. You get married—even if he is the worst man in the world—just so that others can't say no one wants you. You have children, grow old, and spend the end of your days watching passersby from a chair on the sidewalk, pretending to know everything about life yet unable to silence the voice in your heart that says: *"You could try something else."*

A gull approached us, shrieked, and walked away again. It came so close that Astruc put his arm over his eyes to protect himself. That shriek brought me back to reality; I was once again a famous woman, confident in her beauty.

"I want to stop. I cannot continue this life. How much longer can I work as an actress and dancer?"

He was honest in his reply:

"Perhaps another five years or so."

"Then let's end things here."

Astruc took my hand.

"We can't! There are still contracts to fulfill, and I will be fined if we don't fulfill them. What's more, you need to earn a living. You don't want to end your days in that filthy boardinghouse where I found you, do you?"

"We will finish the contracts. You have been good to me, and I won't make you pay for my delusions of grandeur or baseness. But don't worry; I know how I'll keep making a living."

And without giving it much thought, I began to tell him about my life—something that I had kept to myself up until then because it was all just one lie after another. As I spoke, tears began to stream down my face. Astruc asked if I was okay, but I continued to tell him everything and he said nothing, just sat there listening to me in silence.

In finally accepting that I was not at all what I'd thought, I felt I was sinking into a black pit. Suddenly, however, as I faced my wounds and scars, I began to feel stronger. My tears did not come from my eyes, but from a deeper, darker place in my heart, telling me a story that I didn't even fully understand in a voice of its own. I was on a raft, sailing through total darkness, but there, far off on the horizon, was the glow of a lighthouse that would eventually lead me to dry land if the rough seas allowed, and if it was not already too late.

I had never done that before. I thought that speaking about my wounds would only make them more real. And yet the exact opposite was taking place: My tears were healing me.

At times I punched my fists into the gravel beach and my hands bled, but I didn't even feel the pain. I was being healed. I understood why Catholics confess, even though they must know priests share the same sins, or worse. It did not matter who was listening; what mattered was leaving the wound open for the sun to purify and the rainwater to wash. That is what I was doing now, in front of a man with whom I had no intimacy. That was the real reason I was able to speak so freely.

After a long while, after I stopped sobbing and let the sound of the waves soothe me, Astruc took me gently by the arm. He said the last train to Paris would be departing soon and that we'd better hurry. On the way, he told me all the latest news from the art world, such as who was sleeping with whom and who had been fired from what places.

I laughed and asked for more. He was a truly wise and elegant man; he knew that my tears had drained everything out of me and buried it in the sand, where it must remain until the end of time.

"*We are living through* the greatest period in France's history. When did you arrive?"

"During the World's Fair; Paris was different then, more provincial, though it still thought it was the center of the world."

The afternoon sun streamed through the window of the expensive room at the Hotel Élysée Palace. We were surrounded by all the very best France could offer: champagne, absinthe, chocolate, cheese, and the scent of freshly cut flowers. Outside I could see the big tower that now bore the name of its builder, Eiffel.

He also eyed the huge iron structure.

"It wasn't built to remain after the end of the fair.

I hope they move forward quickly with the plans to dismantle that monstrosity."

I could have disagreed, but he'd just submit more arguments and win in the end. So I kept quiet as he spoke of his country's belle époque. Industrial production had tripled, agriculture was now aided by machines capable of single-handedly doing the work of ten men, shops were teeming, and fashion had changed completely. This pleased me very much, as now I had an excuse to go shopping to update my wardrobe at least twice a year.

"Have you noticed that even the food tastes better?"

I had noticed, yes, and I wasn't very pleased about it, because I was starting to gain weight.

"The president told me that the number of bicycles on the streets has increased from three hundred seventy-five thousand at the end of the last century to more than *three million* today. Houses have running water and gas, and people can travel far and wide during their holidays. Coffee consumption has quadrupled, and people can purchase bread without having to queue in front of the bakeries."

Why was he giving this lecture? It was time to yawn and return to playing the "dumb woman."

Adolphe Messimy—former minister of war and now a deputy in the National Assembly—rose from the bed and began to put on his clothes with all his medals and awards. He had a meeting with his old battalion and could not go dressed as a simple civilian.

"Though we loathe the English, they are right about one thing: It's more discreet to go to war in those horrible brown uniforms. We, on the other hand, feel we must die with elegance, in red trousers and caps that just scream to the enemy: 'Hey, point your rifles and cannons over here! Can't you see us?' "

He laughed at his own joke. I also laughed to please him, and then began to get dressed. I had long since lost any illusion of being loved for who I was and now accepted, with a clean conscience, flowers, flattery, and money that fed my ego and my false identity. For certain, I'd go to my grave one day without ever knowing love, but what difference did it make? For me, love and power were the same thing.

However, I wasn't foolish enough to let others realize that. I approached Messimy and gave him a loud peck on his cheek, half of which was covered by whiskers similar to those of my ill-fated husband.

He put a fat envelope with a thousand francs on the table.

"Don't misunderstand me, Mademoiselle. Given that I was just speaking of the country's progress, I believe it's time to help the consumer. I'm an officer who earns a lot and spends little. So I need to contribute something, stimulate consumption."

Again, he laughed at his own joke. He sincerely believed that I loved those medals and his close relationship to the president, whom he made a point to mention every time we met.

If he realized it was all fake, that—for me—love obeyed no rules, perhaps he would pull away and later punish me. He wasn't there just for the sex, but to feel wanted, as a woman's passion could truly arouse the feeling that he was capable of anything.

Yes, love and power were the same thing—and not just for me.

He left and I got dressed leisurely. My next encounter was late at night, outside Paris. I would stop by the hotel, put on my best dress, and go to Neuilly, where my most faithful lover had bought a villa in my name. I thought of also asking him for a car and driver, but figured he would be suspicious.

Of course, I could have been more—shall we say—demanding of him. He was married, a banker with a fine reputation, and the newspapers would have had a ball if I insinuated anything in public. Now they were only interested in my "famous lovers," completely forgetting the extensive body of work I had struggled so hard to create.

During my trial, I heard that someone had been there in the hotel lobby, pretending to read a newspaper but actually watching my every move. As soon as I'd go out, he would rise from his seat and discreetly follow me.

I strolled down the boulevards of the most beautiful city in the world. I saw the overflowing cafés and the increasingly well-dressed people walking from one place to another. As I heard violin music issuing from the doors and windows of the most sophisticated places, I thought how life had been good to me after all. There was no need for blackmail, all I had to do was know how to manage the gifts I'd received and I could grow old in peace. Besides, if I said a word about a single man with whom I'd slept, the others would flee my company for fear of also being blackmailed and exposed.

I had plans to go to the château my banker friend had had built for his "golden years." Poor thing; he was already old, but didn't want to admit it. I would stay there for two or three days riding horses, and by Sunday I could be back in Paris, where I'd go straight to the Longchamp Racecourse and show all those who envied and admired me that I was an excellent horsewoman.

But why not have a nice chamomile tea before night fell? I sat outside a café while people stared at the face and body that was on various postcards scattered throughout the city. I pretended to be lost in a world of reverie, with an air of someone who had more important things to do.

Before I even had the chance to order something, a man approached and complimented my beauty. I reacted with my usual look of ennui and thanked him with a stiff smile, then turned away. But the man did not move.

"A nice cup of coffee will salvage the rest of your day."

I said nothing. He motioned to the waiter and asked him to take my order.

"A chamomile tea, please," I said to the waiter.

The man's French had a thick accent that could have been from Holland or Germany.

He smiled and touched the brim of his hat as if bidding farewell even though he was greeting me. He asked if I would mind if he sat there for a few minutes. I said yes, in fact I would mind. I would rather be alone.

"A woman like Mata Hari is never alone," said the newcomer. The fact that he recognized me struck a chord that can resonate very loudly in any human being: vanity. Still, I did not invite him to sit.

"Maybe you are looking for things you haven't yet found," he continued. "Because after being named the best dressed in the whole city—I read that in a magazine recently—very little remains for you to conquer, isn't that right? And suddenly, life turns into utter boredom."

By the looks of it, he was a devoted fan; how else would he know about things that appeared only in women's magazines? Should I give him a chance? After all, it was still far too early to go to Neuilly for my dinner with the banker.

"Are you having any luck finding something new?" he persisted.

"Of course. I rediscover myself at every turn. And that is what's most interesting in life."

This time, he did not ask again; he simply pulled up a chair and sat down at my table. When the waiter arrived with my tea, he ordered a large cup of coffee for himself, making a gesture that indicated: *I'll get the bill.*

"France is heading for a crisis," he continued. "And it will be very difficult to come out of this one."

Just that afternoon, I had heard exactly the opposite. But it seems every man has an opinion on the economy, a subject that did not interest me in the least.

I decided to play his game for a bit. I parroted everything Messimy had told me about what he called *la belle époque.* He showed no surprise.

"I am not just talking about an economic crisis; I am speaking of a personal crisis, a crisis of values. Do you think people have already grown accustomed to the possibility of having long-distance conversations on that invention brought over by the Americans for the Paris World's Fair? It's now on every corner in Europe.

"For millions of years, man spoke only to what he could see. Suddenly, in just one decade, 'seeing' and 'speaking' have been separated. We think we're used to it, yet we don't realize the immense impact it's had on our reflexes. Our bodies are simply not used to it.

"Frankly, the result is that, when we talk on the telephone, we enter a state that is similar to certain magical trances; we can discover other things about ourselves."

The waiter returned with the bill. The man stopped talking until he had moved away.

"I know you must be tired of seeing these vulgar strip-tease dancers on every corner, each saying she's the successor of the great Mata Hari. But life is like that: No one learns. The Greek philosophers . . . Am I boring you, Mademoiselle?"

I shook my head and he continued.

"Forget about the Greek philosophers. What they said thousands of years ago still applies today. So it's nothing new. Actually, I would like to make you a proposition."

Another one, I thought.

"Here they no longer treat you with the respect you deserve, so maybe you would like to perform in a place where they know you as the greatest dancer of the century? I am talking about Berlin, the city where I'm from."

It was a tempting proposition.

"I can put you in touch with my manager—"

But the newcomer cut me off. "I'd prefer to deal directly with you. Your agent is of a race we—neither the French nor the Germans—don't like very much."

It was a strange business, this hatred for people just because of their religion. I saw it with the Jews, but even earlier, when I was in Java, I heard about the army massacring people just because they worshipped a faceless god and swore that their holy book had been dictated by an angel to some prophet whose name I also can't remember. Someone had given me a copy of this book once, called the Koran. It was just to appreciate the Arabic calligraphy, but still, when my husband arrived home, he took away the gift and had me burn it.

"My partners and I will pay you a handsome sum," the man added, revealing an intriguing amount of money. I asked how much it was in francs and was stunned by his reply. I desired to say yes immediately, but a lady of class does not act on impulse.

"There you will be recognized as you deserve. Paris is always unjust with its children, especially when they cease to be a novelty."

He did not realize he was insulting me, even though I had been thinking that same thing while I was walking. I remembered the day on the beach with Astruc, who would not be able to participate in the agreement. However, I could do nothing that would scare off the prey.

"I'll think about it," I said drily.

We bid each other farewell and he told me where he was staying, saying he would await my reply until the following day, when he had to return to his city. I left the café and went straight to Astruc's office. I confess that seeing all those posters of people just finding their fame made me feel a tremendous sadness. But I could not go back in time.

Astruc welcomed me with the same courtesy as always, as if I were his most important artist. I recounted the conversation I'd had and said that no matter what happened, he would receive his commission.

The only thing he said was: "But right now?"

I didn't quite understand. I thought he was being slightly rude to me.

"Yes, now. I still have much, much more to do onstage."

He nodded in agreement, wished me happiness, and said he didn't need his commission, suggesting that perhaps it was time I start saving my money and stop spending so much on clothes.

I agreed and left. I thought he must still be shaken by what a failure the debut of his theater had been. He must have been on the verge of ruin. Of course, putting on something like *Rite of Spring,* and with a plagiarist like Nijinsky in the lead role, was just asking for the crosswinds to smash one's ship.

The next day I contacted the foreigner and said I accepted his offer, but not before making a series of absurd demands that I was ready to forgo. But to my surprise, he merely called me extravagant and said he agreed to everything, because true artists are like that.

Who was the Mata Hari who embarked that rainy day from one of the city's many train stations? She didn't know what her next step was, or what her destination held in store, only trusted that she was going to a country where the language was similar to her own, and so she would never get lost.

How old was I? Twenty? Twenty-one? I couldn't have been older than twenty-two, though the passport I was carrying with me said I was born on August 7, 1876. As the train made its way to Berlin, the newspaper showed the date July 11, 1914. But I did not want to do the math; I was more interested in what had happened two weeks earlier. The cruel attack in Sarajevo, where Archduke Ferdinand lost his life along with his elegant wife, her only guilt being that she was by his side when a crazy anarchist fired the shots.

In any event, I felt completely different from all the other women in that car. I was an exotic bird traversing an earth ravaged by humanity's poverty of spirit. I was a swan among ducks who refused to grow up, fearing the unknown. I looked at the couples around me and felt completely vulnerable; many men were around me, but there I was, alone, with no one to hold my hand. True, I had turned down many proposals; I had had my experience with that—suffering for someone undeserving and selling my body for the supposed security of a home—in this life and didn't intend to repeat it.

The man next to me, Franz Olav, seemed worried as he looked out the window. I asked what the matter was, but he didn't answer; now that I was under his control, he no longer had to answer anything. All I had to do was dance and dance, even if I was no longer as flexible as I was before. But with a little practice, and thanks to my passion for riding horses, surely I would be ready in time for the premiere. France no longer interested me; it had sucked the very best from me and cast me aside, preferring Russian artists or those born in places like Portugal, Norway, Spain, who repeated the same trick I had used when I arrived. Show them something exotic from your homeland, and the French, always eager for something new, will certainly believe it.

Merely for a short time, but they will believe just the same.

As the train rumbled into Germany, I saw soldiers marching toward the western border. There were battalions and more battalions, gigantic machine guns, and cannons pulled by horses.

Again I tried to make conversation: "What is going on?"

But all I got was a cryptic reply:

"Whatever is going on, I want to know that we can count on your help. Artists are very important at this moment."

He couldn't have been talking about the war, as nothing had been published about it yet— the French papers were much more worried with reporting the latest salon gossip or complaining about some chef who had just lost a government medal. Though our countries hated each other, this was normal.

When a country becomes the most important in the world, there is always a price to pay. England had an empire on which the sun never set, but ask anyone which city they would rather see, London or Paris. I have no doubt the answer would be the city crossed by the River Seine, with its churches, boutiques, theaters, painters, musicians, and—for those a bit more daring—world-famous cabarets like the Folies Bergère, Moulin Rouge, Lido.

You had only to consider what was more important: a tower with a dull clock and a king who never appeared in public or a gigantic steel structure that was the largest vertical tower in the world and which was becoming well known across Europe by the name of its creator, Gustave Eiffel. Or what about the monumental Arc de Triomphe, or the Champs-Élysées, which offered up all the best things money could buy? England also hated France with all its might, but this was no reason for it to prepare its warships.

However, as the train traversed German soil, troops and more troops headed west. I urged Franz again, and received the same cryptic answer.

"I'm ready to help," I said. "But how can I, if I don't even know what this is about?"

For the first time he unglued his eyes from the window and turned to me.

"I don't know. I was hired to bring you to Berlin, to make you dance for our aristocracy, and then one day—I don't have the exact date—go to the Ministry of Foreign Affairs. It was one of your admirers there who gave me the money to hire you, though you're one of the most expensive artists I've ever met. I hope the risk pays off."

Before I bring this chapter of my life to a close, my dearest, detested Mr. Clunet, I would like to speak a bit more about myself, because that was why I began writing these pages, which have turned into a record where, in many parts, my memory may have betrayed me.

Do you really think—in your heart—that if they were to choose someone to spy for Germany, France, or even Russia, they would choose someone who was constantly watched by the public? Does that not seem utterly ridiculous to you?

When I took that train to Berlin, I thought I had left my past behind. With each kilometer, I moved farther away from everything I had experienced, even the good memories like the discovery of what

I was capable of doing onstage and off and the moments in which every street and every party in Paris were a great novelty. Now I understand that I cannot run from myself. In 1914, instead of returning to Holland, it would have been very easy to change my name again, find someone to take care of what was left of my soul, and go to one of the many places in this world where my face was unknown to start anew.

But that meant living the rest of my life split in two: as a woman who could be anything and one who was never anything, one who wouldn't have even a single story to tell her children and grandchildren. Though at the moment I am a prisoner, my spirit remains free. While everyone is fighting a never-ending battle to see who will survive amid so much bloodshed, I don't need to fight anymore, only wait for people I've never met to decide who I am. If they find me guilty, one day the truth will come out, and a mantle of shame will be draped over their heads, and that of their children, their grandchildren, their country.

I sincerely believe that the president is a man of honor.

I believe that my friends, always gentle and willing to help me when I had everything, are still by my side now that I have nothing. The day has just dawned, and I can hear birds and noise from the kitchen downstairs. The rest of the prisoners are sleeping, some afraid, some resigned to their fate. I slept until the first ray of sun, and that ray of sun, though it did not enter my cell, only showed its strength in the sliver of sky I can see, brought me hope for justice.

I don't know why life made me go through so much in so little time.

To see if I could withstand the hard times.

To see what I was made of.

To give me experience.

But there were other methods, other ways to achieve this. It did not need to drown me in the darkness of my own soul or make me cross through this forest filled with wolves and other wild animals without a single hand to guide me.

The only thing I know is that this forest, however frightening it may be, has an end, and I intend to reach its other side. I will be generous in victory and will not accuse those who lied so much about me.

Do you know what I am going to do now, before

I hear the footsteps in the corridor and the arrival of my breakfast? I am going to dance. I am going to remember every musical note and move my body to the rhythm, because it shows me who I am—a free woman!

Because that's what I always sought: freedom. I did not seek love, though it has come and gone. Because of love, I have done things, things I shouldn't have, and traveled to places where people were lying in wait for me.

But I do not want to rush my own story; life is moving very quickly and I have struggled to keep up with it since that morning I arrived in Berlin.

The theater was surrounded. The show was interrupted during a moment of great concentration, when I was giving my best despite being out of practice. German soldiers took the stage and said that all performances in concert halls were canceled until further notice.

One of them read a statement aloud:

"These are the words of our kaiser: '*We are living a dark moment in the history of our country, which is surrounded by enemies. We shall need to unsheathe our swords. I hope we may use them well and with dignity.*'"

I couldn't understand a thing. I went to the dressing room, slipped my robe over what little clothing I had on, and saw Franz enter the door, panting.

"You need to leave or you'll be arrested."

"Leave? And go where? Besides, don't I have an appointment tomorrow morning with someone from the German Ministry of Foreign Affairs?"

"Everything is canceled," he said, doing nothing to conceal his concern. "You're lucky you're a citizen of a neutral country—that's where you should go immediately."

I thought about everything in my life, except returning to my home country, the one place that had been so difficult to leave.

Franz took a wad of marks from his pocket and placed them in my hands.

"Forget about the six-month contract we signed with the Metropol-Theater. This was all the money I was able to scrounge from the theater safe. Leave immediately. I'll take care of sending your clothes later, if I'm still alive. Because, unlike you, I've just been called up by the military."

I understood less and less.

"The world's gone mad," he said, pacing.

"The death of a relative, no matter how close, is no good reason for sending people to their deaths. But the generals rule the world and they want to continue what we didn't finish when France was shamefully defeated more than forty years ago. They think they're still living back then and decided amongst themselves to avenge their humiliation. They want to keep France from gaining strength, and there's every indication that with each passing day, it really is growing stronger. That's why this is happening: Kill the snake before it becomes too strong and strangles us."

"Are you saying we're heading for war? Is that why so many soldiers were traveling a week ago?"

"Exactly. The game of chess has become more complicated because our rulers are bound by alliances. It's too tiresome for me to explain. But right now, as we speak, our armies are invading Belgium, Luxembourg has already surrendered, and now they are moving toward the industrial regions of France with seven well-armed divisions. While the French were enjoying life, we were looking for a pretext. While the French were building the Eiffel Tower, our men were investing in cannons. I don't believe all this will last very long; after some deaths on both sides, peace always wins out. But until then you'll have to take refuge in your own country and wait for everything to calm down."

Franz's words surprised me; he seemed genuinely interested in my well-being. I drew near and touched his face.

"Don't worry, everything is going to be fine."

"It's not going to be fine," he replied, tossing my hand aside. "And the thing I wanted most is lost forever."

He took the hand he had so violently brushed away.

"When I was younger, my parents made me learn piano. I always hated it, and as soon as I left home, I forgot it all, except one thing: The most beautiful melody in the world will become a monstrosity if the strings are out of tune.

"I was in Vienna, completing my mandatory military service, when we had two days of R & R. I saw a poster of a girl who, even without ever seeing her in person, immediately aroused something no man should ever feel: love at first sight. When I entered the crowded theater and bought a ticket that cost more than I earned in a whole week, I saw that everything inside me that was out of tune—my relationships with my parents, the army, my country, the world—suddenly harmonized just by watching this girl dance. It wasn't the exotic music, or the eroticism onstage and in the audience, it was the girl."

I knew who he was talking about, but didn't want to interrupt.

"That girl was you. I should have told you all this earlier, but I thought there would be time. Today I am a successful theater manager, perhaps because of everything I saw that night in Vienna. Tomorrow I will report to the captain in charge of my unit. I went to Paris several times to see your shows. I saw that, no matter what you did, Mata Hari was losing ground to a bunch of people who didn't deserve to be called 'dancers' or 'artists.' I decided to bring you to a place where people would appreciate your work; and I did all of it for love, only for love . . . an unrequited love, but what does that matter? What really counts is being close to the one you love; that was my goal.

"One day before I could work up the courage to approach you in Paris, an embassy official contacted me. He said you kept company with a deputy who, according to our intelligence service, would be the next minister of war."

"But that's all over now."

"According to our intelligence service, he will return to the position he occupied previously. I'd met with that embassy official many times before—we used to drink together and frequented the Paris nightlife. On one of those nights, I drank a little too much and talked about you for hours on end. He knew I was in love and asked me to bring you here, because we were going to need your services very soon."

"My services?"

"As someone who has access to the government's inner circle."

The word he was trying to say, but didn't have the courage to voice, was "spy." Something I would never do in all my life. As I'm sure you remember, honorable Mr. Clunet, I said as much during that farce of a trial: "A prostitute, yes. A spy, never!"

"That's why you have to leave this theater straightaway and go directly to Holland. The money I gave you is more than enough. Soon this journey will be impossible. Or, more terrible yet, if it were still possible, that would mean we'd managed to infiltrate someone into Paris."

I was quite frightened, but not enough to give

him a kiss or thank him for what he was doing for me.

I was going to lie and say I would be waiting for him when the war was over, but honesty has a way of dissolving lies.

Pianos should never go out of tune. The true sin is something different than what we've been taught; the true sin is living so far removed from absolute harmony. That is more powerful than the truths and lies we tell every day. I turned to him and kindly asked him to leave, as I needed to get dressed. And I said:

"Sin was not created by God; it was created by us when we tried to transform what was inevitable into something subjective. We ceased to see the whole and came to see just one part; and that part is loaded with guilt, rules, good versus evil, and each side thinking it's right."

I surprised myself with my words. Maybe fear had affected me more than I thought. But my head felt far away.

"I have a friend who is the German consul in your country. He can help you rebuild your life. But be careful: Like me, it's quite possible he will try to get you to help our war effort."

Once again he avoided the word "spy." I was an experienced enough woman to escape these traps. How many times had I done it in my relationships with men?

He led me to the door and took me to the train station. Along the way we passed a huge demonstration in front of the kaiser's palace, where men of all ages, fists clenched in the air, shouted:

"Germany above all!"

Franz accelerated the car.

"If someone stops us, keep quiet and I'll handle the conversation. But if they ask you something, just say 'yes' or 'no.' Look bored and don't dare speak the enemy's language. When you get to the station, show no fear, not under any circumstances; continue to be who you are."

Be who I am? How could I be true to myself if I didn't even know exactly who I was? The dancer who took Europe by storm? The housewife who humiliated herself in the Dutch East Indies? The lover of powerful men? The woman the press called a "vulgar artist," despite, just a short time before, admiring and idolizing her?

We arrived at the station. Franz gave me a polite kiss on the hand and asked me to take the first train. It was the first time in my life I had traveled without luggage; even when I arrived in Paris I was carrying something.

As paradoxical as it may seem, this gave me an enormous sense of freedom. Soon I would have my clothes with me, but in the meantime, I was assuming a role life had thrust upon me: that of a woman who has absolutely nothing, a princess far from her castle, comforted by the fact that soon she will return.

After buying my ticket to Amsterdam, I found I still had a few hours until the train departed. Despite trying to appear discreet, I noticed everyone was looking at me, but it was a different kind of look—not of admiration or envy, but curiosity. The platforms were buzzing and, unlike me, everyone seemed to be carrying their entire homes in suitcases, bundles, and carpetbags. I overheard a mother telling her daughter the same thing Franz had told me shortly before: *"If a guard appears, speak in German."*

They weren't exactly people who were thinking of going to the countryside, but possible "spies," refugees returning to their countries.

I decided not to speak to anyone and to avoid all

eye contact, but even so, an older man approached and asked: "Won't you come dance with us?"

Had he uncovered my identity?

"We're over there, at the end of the platform. Come!"

I followed him blindly, knowing I would be better protected if I mixed with strangers. I soon found myself surrounded by Gypsies and, instinctively, clutched my purse closer to my body. There was fear in their eyes, but they did not seem to give in to it, as though they were accustomed to having to change expressions. Clapping their hands, they had formed a circle, and three women danced in the middle.

"Do you want to dance, too?" asked the man who had brought me there.

I said I had never danced in my life. He insisted, but I explained that, even if I wanted to try, my dress did not allow me freedom of movement. He seemed satisfied, began to clap his hands, and asked me to do the same.

"We are Roma from the Balkans," he said to me. "From what I've heard, that's where the war started. We have to get out of here as soon as possible."

I was going to explain that no, the war hadn't

started in the Balkans, and that it was all a pretext to ignite a powder keg that had been ready to
explode for many years. But it was better to keep my
mouth shut, like Franz recommended.

". . . but this war will come to an end," said a
woman with black hair and eyes, much prettier than
her simple clothes might suggest. "All wars come to
an end. Many will profit at the expense of the dead,
and, in the meantime, we will keep on traveling far
away from the conflicts while the conflicts insist
upon pursuing us."

Nearby, a group of children played, as if travel
was always an adventure and none of this was
important. For them, dragons were in constant battle, and knights fought one another while dressed
in steel and armed with large lances. It was a world
where, if one boy didn't chase after another, it would
be an extremely dull place.

The Gypsy woman who had spoken to me went
to them and asked them to quiet down, because
they shouldn't be so conspicuous. None of them
paid any attention.

A beggar, who seemed to know every passerby on the main street, sang:

> *The caged bird may sing of freedom, but it will still live*
> *in prison.*
> *Thea agreed to live in the cage, then wanted to escape,*
> *but no one helped, because no one understood.*

I had no idea who Thea was; all I knew was I had to get to the consulate as soon as possible to introduce myself to Karl Kramer, the only person I knew in The Hague. I had spent the night in a third-rate hotel, afraid someone would recognize me and kick me out. The Hague was teeming with people who

117

seemed to be living on another planet. Apparently, news of the war had not yet reached the city, stuck at the border along with thousands of other refugees, deserters, French citizens fearing reprisals, and Belgians fleeing the battlefront, all seemingly waiting for the impossible.

For the first time I was happy to have been born in Leeuwarden and hold a Dutch passport. My Dutch passport had been my salvation. As I waited to be searched—glad not to have any luggage—a man I didn't even get a good look at tossed me an envelope. It was addressed to someone, but the officer in charge of the border saw what had happened. He opened the letter, closed it, and then handed it to me without comment. Immediately thereafter, he called over his German counterpart and pointed toward the man, who had already disappeared into the darkness:

"A deserter."

The German officer ran after him; the war had barely started and already people were beginning to flee? I saw him raise his rifle and point it toward the running figure. I looked the other way when he fired. I want to live the rest of my life believing he managed to escape.

The letter was addressed to a woman and I thought perhaps he was hoping I would put it in the mail when I got to The Hague.

I will get out of here, no matter the price—even if it is my own life—for I might be shot as a deserter if they catch me on the way. It would seem the war is starting now; the first French troops appeared on the other side and were immediately wiped out by a single burst of gunfire fired on the captain's orders. Supposedly, this will all end soon, but even so, there is blood on my hands, and I will never be able to do what I've done a second time; I cannot march with my battalion to Paris, as everyone notes with excitement. I cannot celebrate the victories that await us, because this all seems mad. The more I think, the less I understand what is happening. No one says anything, because I believe no one knows the answer.

Incredible as it may seem, we still have postal service. I could have used it, but from what I've heard, all correspondence passes through censors prior to being sent. This letter is not to say how much I love you—you already know this. Nor is it to speak of the bravery of our soldiers, a fact known throughout Germany. This letter is my last will and testament. I

*am writing under the same tree where, six months ago,
I asked for your hand in marriage and you said yes. We
made plans; your parents helped with the trousseau,
I looked for a house with an extra room, where we
could have our first, long-awaited son. Now I am in
the same place after three days spent digging trenches
while covered from head to toe in mud and the blood of
five or six people I had never seen before, who never did
me any harm. They call it a "just war" to protect our
dignity, as if a battlefield were any place for that.*

*The more I watch the first shots and smell the blood
of the first casualties, the more I am convinced that
human dignity cannot coexist with this. I must end
now because they just called for me. But as soon as the
sun sets, I am leaving here—for Holland or my death.*

*I think that with each passing day I will be less
able to describe what is happening. Therefore, I prefer
to leave here tonight and find a good soul to post this
envelope for me.*

With all my love,
Jorn

As soon as I arrived in Amsterdam the gods con-
spired for me to find one of my hairdressers from

Paris, wearing a war uniform, on the platform. He was known for his technique for applying henna to women's hair so that the color always looked natural and pleasing to the eye.

"Van Staen!"

He looked toward the sound of my cry; his face was overcome with bewilderment, and, immediately, he started to turn away.

"Maurice, it's me, Mata Hari!"

But he continued to hurry away. I was outraged. A man to whom I'd paid thousands of francs was now running from me? I began walking toward him, and his pace quickened. I quickened mine as well, and he started to run, until a gentleman who had witnessed the whole scene took him by the arm and said, "That woman is calling your name!"

He resigned himself to his fate. He stopped and waited for me to approach. In a low voice, he asked me not to mention his name again.

"What are you doing here?"

He told me then that in the early days of the war he'd decided to enlist to defend Belgium, his country, while imbued with patriotic spirit. But as soon as he heard the crack of the first cannons, he immediately crossed to Holland and sought asylum. I feigned a certain disdain.

"I need you to do my hair."

In fact, I desperately needed to regain some self-esteem until my luggage arrived. The money Franz had given me was enough to keep me going for one or two months while I thought of a way to return to Paris. I asked where I could stay—temporarily, since I had at least one friend there, and he would help me until things calmed down.

One year later, I was settled in The Hague, thanks to my friendship with a banker I'd met in Paris. He'd rented a house for me where we used to meet. At one point, he stopped paying the rent without saying exactly why, but perhaps it was because he considered my tastes, as he'd once told me, "expensive and extravagant." In reply, I told him: "Extravagant is a man ten years my senior wanting to regain his lost youth between the legs of a woman."

He took that as a personal insult—which was my intention—and asked me to move out of the house. The Hague had already been a dreary place when I'd visited as a child; now—with rationing and the absence of nightlife due to the war raging in neighboring countries with increasing fury—it had turned into an old-age home, a nest of spies, and a massive bar where the wounded and deserters went to drown their sorrows and get into brawls that usually ended in death. I tried to organize a series of theatrical performances based on ancient Egyptian dances—since no one knew how they danced in ancient Egypt and the critics couldn't dispute its authenticity, I could do this easily. But theaters had little in the way of audiences and no one accepted my offer.

Paris seemed like a distant dream. But it was the only true north in my life, the only city where I felt like a human being and everything that means. There, I was allowed both what was accepted and what was sinful. The clouds were different, the people walked with elegance, and conversations were a thousand times more interesting than the dull discussions in The Hague's hair salons, where people hardly spoke for fear of being heard by someone and reported to the police for denigrating and undermining the country's neutral image. For a while, I tried to inquire about Maurice Van Staen. I asked a few school friends who had moved to Amsterdam about him, but he had seemingly vanished from the face of the earth with his henna techniques and his ridiculous fake French accent.

My only way out now was to get the Germans to take me to Paris. And so I decided to meet with Franz's friend, first sending a note explaining who I was and requesting his help to realize my dream of returning to the city where I had spent much of my life. I had lost the weight I'd gained during that long and dark period; my clothes never made it to Holland and, even if they arrived now, they would no longer be welcome. The magazines showed that the fashion had changed, so my "benefactor" had bought me all new things. Not of Parisian quality, of course, but at least the seams didn't rip at the first movement.

When I entered the office, I saw a man surrounded by every luxury denied to the Dutch: imported cigarettes and cigars, libations from the four corners of Europe, cheeses and charcuterie that had been rationed in the city's markets. Sitting behind a mahogany desk with gold filigree was a well-dressed man, more polite than any of the Germans I had ever met. We exchanged pleasantries and he asked me why it had taken me so long to visit him.

"I didn't know you were expecting me. Franz . . ."

"He told me you would come one year ago."

He got up, asked what I would like to drink. I chose aniseed liqueur, which the consul served himself in Bohemian crystal glasses.

"Unfortunately, Franz is no longer with us; he died during a cowardly attack by the French."

From the little I knew, the rapid German onslaught in August 1914 had been held at the Belgian border. The idea of reaching Paris quickly, as the letter I had been entrusted with read, was now a distant dream.

"We had everything so well planned! Am I boring you with this?"

I asked him to continue. Yes, I was bored, but I wanted to get to Paris as soon as possible and I knew I needed his help. Ever since I'd arrived in The Hague I had to learn something extremely difficult: the art of patience.

The consul noted my look of ennui and tried to summarize what had happened as much as possible. They had sent seven divisions to the West and advanced onto French territory with speed, getting as far as fifty kilometers from Paris. But the generals had no idea how the General Command had organized the offensive, and that brought a retreat to where they were now, close to a territory bordering Belgium. For practically one year, they hadn't been able to move without soldiers on one side or the other being massacred. But no one surrendered.

"When this war is over, I'm sure that every village in France, no matter how small, will have a monument to their dead. They keep sending more and more people to be sliced in half by our cannons."

The expression "sliced in half" shocked me, and he noticed my air of disgust.

"Let's just say that the sooner this nightmare is over, the better. Even with England on their side, and even though our stupid allies—the Austrians— have their hands full trying to halt the Russian advance, we will win in the end. For this, however, we need your help."

My help? To stop a war that, according to what I'd read or heard at the few dinners I attended in The Hague, had already cost the lives of thousands? What was he getting at?

Suddenly I remembered Franz's warning, which reverberated inside my head: *Do not accept anything Kramer might propose.*

My life, however, could not get any worse. I was desperate for money, with no place to sleep and debts piling up. I knew what he was going to propose, but I was sure I could find my way out of the trap. I had already escaped many in my life.

I asked him to go straight to the point. Karl Kramer's body stiffened and his tone changed abruptly. I was no longer a guest to whom he owed a bit of courtesy before addressing more important matters; he began to treat me as his subordinate.

"From your note, I understand you wish to go to Paris. I can get you there. I can also get you an allowance of twenty thousand francs."

"That's not enough," I replied.

"This amount will be adjusted as the quality of your work becomes apparent and the probationary period is completed. Don't worry; our pockets are lined with money when it comes to this. In return, I need any sort of information you can get in the circles you frequent."

Frequented, I thought to myself. I didn't know how I would be received in Paris after a year and a half; especially when the last news anyone had of me was that I was traveling to Germany for a series of shows.

Kramer took three small flasks from a drawer and handed them to me.

"This is invisible ink. Whenever you have news, use it, and send it to Captain Hoffmann, who is in charge of your case. Never sign your name."

He took a list, scanned it up and down, and made a mark next to something.

"Your codename will be H21. Remember that: You will always sign 'H21.' "

I wasn't sure if it was meant to be funny, dangerous, or stupid. They could have at least chosen a better name, and not an abbreviation that sounded like a seat number on a train.

From the other drawer he took twenty thousand francs in cash, and handed me the stack of notes.

"My subordinates, in the front room, will take care of details like passports and safe-conducts. As you might imagine, it is impossible to cross a border during a war. So the only alternative is to travel first to London and, from there, to the city where, soon, we shall march under the imposing—but foolishly named—Arc de Triomphe."

I left Kramer's office with everything I needed: money, two passports, and safe-conducts. When I crossed the first bridge, I emptied the bottles of invisible ink—it was something for children who like to play war but never imagined they would be taken so seriously by adults. Next I went to the French consulate and asked the chargé d'affaires to contact the head of counterespionage. He responded with disbelief.

"And why do you want that?"

I said it was a private matter and I would never speak with subordinates about it. I must have seemed serious, since soon I was on the telephone with his superior, who answered without revealing his name. I said I had just been recruited by German intelligence, gave him all the details, and asked for a meeting with him as soon as I got to Paris, my next destination. He asked my name, and said he was a fan of my work and that they would be sure to contact me as soon as I reached the City of Light. I explained that I did not yet know in which hotel I would be staying.

"Don't worry; it is precisely our job to find out these sorts of things."

Life had become interesting again, though I wouldn't discover how interesting until later on. To my surprise, when I arrived back at the hotel, there was an envelope asking me to contact one of the directors of the Royal Theatre. My proposal was accepted, and I was invited to perform the historical Egyptian dances to the public, provided they involved no nudity. I thought it was too much of a coincidence, but I did not know if it was help from the Germans or the French.

I decided to accept. I divided the Egyptian dances into Virginity, Passion, Chastity, and Fidelity. Local newspapers spun praise, but after eight performances I was once again bored to death and dreaming of the day I would make my big return to Paris.

In Amsterdam, where I had to wait eight hours for a connection that would take me to England, I decided to take a little walk. Again I ran into the beggar who had sung those strange verses about Thea. I was going to continue on my way, but he interrupted his song.

"Why are you being followed?"

"Because I am beautiful, seductive, and famous," I replied.

But he told me it wasn't those kinds of people who were after me, but two men who, as soon as they'd noticed he'd seen them, mysteriously disappeared.

I couldn't remember the last time I talked to a beggar; it was unacceptable for a lady of high society, though those who envied me still considered me an artist or a prostitute.

"It may not seem it, but here you're in paradise. It may be boring, but what paradise isn't? I know you are likely in search of adventure, and I hope you'll forgive my impertinence, but people are usually ungrateful for what they have."

I thanked him for the advice and went on my way. What kind of paradise was this, where nothing, absolutely nothing, interesting happened? I was not looking for happiness, but what the French called *la vraie vie*, a true life, with its moments of inexpressible beauty and deep depression, with its loyalties and betrayals, with its fears and moments of peace. When the beggar told me I was being followed, I imagined I was playing a much more important role than any of the ones I had played before: I was someone who could change the fate of the world, make France win the war while I pretended I was spying for the Germans. Men think God is a mathematician, but He is not. If anything, God would be a chess player, anticipating His opponent's next move and preparing His strategy to defeat him.

And that was me, Mata Hari, for whom every

moment of light and every moment of darkness meant the same thing. I had survived my marriage, the loss of custody of my daughter—though I'd heard, through third parties, that she kept one of my photos glued to her lunch box—and at no point did I complain or stand still in one place. As I was throwing stones with Astruc on the coast of Normandy, I realized that I had always been a warrior, facing my battles without any bitterness; they were part of life.

My eight-hour wait at the station passed quickly, and soon I was back on the train that took me to Brighton. When I landed in England I was subjected to a quick interrogation; apparently, I was already a marked woman, perhaps because I was traveling alone, perhaps for being who I was, or, what seemed most likely, the French secret service had seen me enter the German consulate and warned all its allies. No one knew about my telephone call and my devotion to the country where I was headed.

I would make a lot of trips over the next two years: traveling across countries I'd never before visited, returning to Germany to see if I could get my things, and being harshly interrogated by British officials even though everyone, absolutely everyone, knew I was working for France. I continued to meet the most interesting of men while dining in the most famous restaurants, and finally, I crossed glances with my one true love, a Russian who had been blinded by the mustard gas used so indiscriminately in this war and for whom I was willing to do anything.

I risked everything and went to Vittel because of him. My life had taken on new meaning. Every night when we would go to bed, I used to recite a passage from Song of Songs.

At night, in my bed, I looked for the one my soul loves;
I looked for him, but could not find him.

So I will rise and go around the city; in the streets and
in the squares I will look for the one my soul loves;
I looked for him, but could not find him.

The watchmen who go around the city found me;
I asked them: have you seen the one my soul loves?

I stood aside and then I found the one my soul loves;
I held him close and wouldn't let him go.

And when he writhed in pain, I would stay up all night nursing his eyes and the burns on his body.

The moment I saw him sitting there on the witness stand, saying he would never fall in love with a woman twenty years his senior, the sharpest of swords pierced my heart; his only interest was in having someone to tend his wounds.

And from what you told me later, Mr. Clunet, it was that fateful pursuit of a pass to allow me to go to Vittel that aroused the suspicions of that damned Ladoux.

From here, Mr. Clunet, I have nothing to add to this story. You know exactly what happened, and how it happened.

And on behalf of all that I've suffered unjustly, the humiliations I am forced to endure, the public defamation I suffered before the judges of the Third War Council, and the lies on both sides—as if the Germans and the French, who are killing each other, couldn't leave a woman whose greatest sin was having a free mind in a world where people are becoming increasingly closed-off well enough alone—on behalf of all this, Mr. Clunet, if my final appeal to the president is refused, I ask you, please, to save this letter and deliver it to my daughter, Non, when she is old enough to understand everything that has happened.

Once I was on a beach in Normandy with my then agent, Monsieur Astruc. I've seen him only once since I came back to Paris, and he said the country was undergoing a wave of anti-Semitism and he could not be seen in my company. He told me about a writer, Oscar Wilde. It was not hard to find the play he had mentioned, *Salome*, but no one had dared invest a single cent into putting on what I was about to produce. Though penniless, I still knew influential people.

Why do I bring this up? How did I wind up interested in the work of this English writer who spent his last days here in Paris, was buried without any friends to attend the funeral, and whose only crime was to have been the lover of a man? Would that this were also my condemnation, because I have been in the beds of famous men and their wives, all in the insatiable pursuit of pleasure. No one ever accused me, of course, because then they would be my witnesses.

But back to the English writer, now cursed in

his country and ignored in ours. During my constant travel, I read a lot of his work for the theater and discovered that he had also written stories for children.

A student wishes to ask his beloved to dance, but she refuses, saying she would only accept if he brought her a red rose. It so happened that in the place where the student lived, all the roses were yellow or white.

The nightingale heard the conversation. Seeing his sorrow, she decided to help the poor boy. First, she thought of singing something beautiful, but soon concluded that it would be much worse—in addition to being alone, he would be melancholy.

A passing butterfly asked what was going on.

"He is suffering for love. He needs to find a red rose."

"How ridiculous to suffer for love," said the butterfly.

But the nightingale was determined to help him. In the middle of a huge garden there was a rosebush full of roses.

"Give me a red rose, please."

But the rosebush said it was impossible, and for him to find another—its roses were once red, but now they had become white.

The nightingale did as she was told. She flew far away and found the old rosebush. "I need a red flower," she asked.

"I'm too old for that" was the answer. "The winter has chilled my veins, the sun faded my petals."

"Just one," begged the nightingale. "There must be a way!"

Yes, there was a way. But it was so terrible that she did not want to tell.

"I'm not afraid. Tell me what I can do to get a red rose. A single red rose."

"Come back at night and sing the most beautiful melody that nightingales know while pressing your breast against one of my thorns. The blood will rise through my sap and color the rose."

And the nightingale did that that night, convinced it was worth sacrificing her life in the name of Love. As soon as the moon appeared she pressed her breast against the thorn and began to sing. First she sang of a man and a woman who fall in love. Then how love justifies any sacrifice. And so, as the moon crossed the sky, the nightingale sang and the most beautiful rose of the rosebush was being crimsoned by her blood.

"Faster," said the rosebush at one point. "The sun will rise soon."

"The nightingale pressed her breast closer still and at that moment the thorn reached her heart. Still, she continued to sing until the work was complete.

Exhausted, and knowing she was about to die, she took the most beautiful of all the red roses and went to give it to the student. She arrived at his window, set down the flower, and died.

The student heard the noise, opened the window, and there was the thing he had dreamed of most in the world. The sun was rising; he took the rose and raced off to the house of his beloved.

"Here's what you asked of me," he said, sweating and happy at the same time.

"It is not exactly what I wanted," answered

the girl. "It is too big and will overshadow my dress. Besides, I have received another proposal for the ball tonight."

Distraught, the boy left and threw the rose into the gutter, where it was immediately crushed by a passing carriage. And he returned to his books, which had never asked him for anything he could not provide.

That was my life; I am the nightingale who gave everything and died while doing so.

Sincerely,
Mata Hari

(Formerly known by the name chosen by her parents, Margaretha Zelle, and then forced to adopt her married name, Madame MacLeod, and finally convinced by the Germans, in exchange for a measly twenty thousand francs, to sign everything as H21.)

Part III

Dear Mata Hari,

Although you do not yet know it, your request for pardon was denied by the president. Therefore, early tomorrow morning I will go to meet you and this shall be the last time we will see each other.

I have eleven long hours before me and I know I will not be able to sleep a single second tonight. Therefore, I am writing you a letter, which will never be read by the person for whom it was intended, but I plan to present it as a final piece of evidence in the investigation; even though this may be absolutely useless from a legal standpoint, I hope to at least recover your reputation while I am still alive.

I do not intend to prove my incompetence with this defense, because I was not in fact the terrible lawyer that you often accused me of being in your many letters. I just want to relive—if only to absolve myself of a sin I did not commit—my ordeal of the past few months. It is an ordeal that I have not lived alone; I was in every way trying to save the woman I once loved, though I never admitted it.

This is an ordeal that is being lived by the entire nation; these days there is not a single family in this country who has not lost a son at the battle-front. And because of that, we commit injustices, atrocities, things I never imagined happening in my country. As I write this, several battles with no end are being waged just two hundred kilometers from here. The biggest and bloodiest of them began with a naïveté on our part; we thought two hundred thousand brave soldiers would be able to defeat more than a million Germans who marched with tanks and heavy artillery toward the capital. But despite having resisted bravely, despite massive bloodshed and thousands of dead and wounded, the war front remains exactly where it stood in 1914, when the Germans initiated the hostilities.

Dear Mata Hari, your biggest mistake was having found the wrong man to do the right thing. Georges Ladoux, the head of counterespionage, who contacted you as soon as you returned to Paris, was a marked man by the government. He was one of those responsible for the Dreyfus case, a miscarriage of justice that still shames us today—condemning an innocent man to degradation and exile. After he was unmasked, he tried to justify his actions by saying his work "was not limited to knowing the enemy's next steps, but preventing him from undermining the morale of our friends." He sought a promotion, which was denied. He became a bitter man who urgently needed a cause célèbre to make him well regarded once again in government halls. And who better for that than a well-known actress, envied by officers' wives and hated by the elite who, years before, used to deify her?

The people cannot think only of the deaths taking place in Verdun, Marne, Somme—they need to be distracted by some kind of victory. And Ladoux, knowing this, began to weave his degrading web the moment he first saw you. He described your first meeting in his notes:

"She entered my office as someone enters a stage, parading around in formal wear and trying to impress me. I did not invite her to sit, but she pulled up a chair and settled in across my desk. After telling me the proposition the German consul made her in The Hague, she said she was ready to work for France. She also ridiculed my agents that were following her, saying, 'Can't your friends downstairs leave me alone for a while? Every time I exit my hotel, they go in and turn the entire room upside down. I can't go to a café without them occupying the next table and this has frightened away the friendships I've cultivated for so long. Now my friends no longer want to be seen with me.'

"I asked her how she would like to serve the country. She replied petulantly: 'You know how. To the Germans I'm H21. Perhaps the French have better taste in choosing names for those who secretly serve the country.'

"I countered in such a way that my words had a double meaning: 'We all know you have a reputation for being expensive in everything you do. How much will this cost?'

" 'All or nothing' was her answer.

"As soon as she left, I asked my secretary to send me the 'Mata Hari dossier.' After reading all the material collected—which had cost us a fortune in man-hours—I could not find anything incriminating. Apparently, the woman was smarter than my agents and had managed to well conceal her nefarious activities."

In other words, even though you were guilty, they could find nothing to incriminate you. The agents continued to file their daily reports; when you went to Vittel with that Russian boyfriend blinded by mustard gas in one of the German attacks, the collection of "reports" bordered on the ridiculous.

People at the hotel tend to always see her accompanied by the war invalid, possibly twenty years her junior. By her exuberance and way of walking, we are certain she uses drugs, probably morphine or cocaine.

She mentioned to one of the guests that she was a member of the Dutch royal family. To another, she said she had a château in Neuilly.

Once when we went out for dinner and returned to work, she was singing in the main hall for a group of youth and we are almost certain her sole objective was to corrupt those innocent girls and boys who, by then, knew they were before the woman they deemed the "great star of the Parisian stage."

When her lover returned to the front, she stayed in Vittel for two more weeks, always going for walks, lunching, and dining alone. We could not detect any contact by an enemy agent, but who would stay at a spa hotel by themselves unless they had dubious interests? Although she was under our watch twenty-four hours a day, she must have found a way to circumvent our surveillance.

And that was when, my dear Mata Hari, the vilest blow of all was struck. You were also being followed by the Germans—who were more discreet and more efficient. From the day of your visit to Captain Ladoux, they had come to the conclusion that you intended to be a double agent. While you strolled about in Vittel, Consul Kramer, who had recruited you in The Hague, was under interrogation in Berlin. They wanted to know about the twenty thousand francs spent on a person whose profile could not be more different than that of a traditional spy—usually discreet and virtually invisible. Why had he called on someone so famous to help Germany in its war effort? Was he also in cahoots with the French? How, after so long, had agent H21 not produced a SINGLE report? "Every now and then she was approached by an agent—usually in public transport—who asked for at least one piece of information, but she would smile seductively and say she had not yet obtained anything."

In Madrid, however, they managed to intercept a letter you sent to the head of counterespionage, that wretched Ladoux, which recounts in detail a meeting with a German high official who had finally managed to circumvent their surveillance and approach you.

"He asked me what I had obtained, if I had sent any messages in invisible ink, and if perhaps something had got lost along the way. I said no. He asked me for a name and I said I had slept with Alfred Kiepert.

"Then, in a fit of rage, he yelled at me, saying

he was not interested in knowing who I'd slept with, or he would be required to fill out pages and pages with the names of English, French, Germans, Dutch, and Russians. I ignored the attack, and he calmed down and offered me cigarettes. I began toying with my legs seductively. Thinking he was before a woman with a brain the size of a pea, he blurted out: 'I'm sorry for my behavior, I'm tired. I need to focus all of my concentration to organize the arrival of ammunition that the Germans and Turks are sending to the coast of Morocco.' Also, I demanded the five thousand francs that Kramer owed me; he said he had no authority to do so and that he would ask the German consulate in The Hague to handle the matter. 'We always pay what we owe,' he said."

The Germans' suspicions were finally confirmed. We don't know what happened to Consul Kramer, but Mata Hari was definitely a double agent who, until then, had not provided any such information. We have a radio surveillance post at the top of the Eiffel Tower, but most of the information that is exchanged between them is in encrypted form, and impossible to read. Ladoux seemed to read their reports and not believe anything; I never knew if he sent someone to check on the arrival of ammunition on the shores of Morocco. But suddenly a telegram was sent from Madrid to Berlin in a code they knew had been already deciphered by the French, and it became the centerpiece of the prosecution, even though it said nothing beyond your nom de guerre.

AGENT H21 WAS ADVISED OF ARRIVAL OF SUBMARINE ON THE COAST OF MOROCCO AND SHOULD ASSIST IN THE TRANSPORT OF AMMUNITION TO MARNE. SHE IS TRAVELING TO PARIS, WHERE SHE WILL ARRIVE TOMORROW.

Ladoux now had all the evidence he needed to incriminate you. But I was not so foolish as to think a simple telegram could convince the military tribunal of your guilt, especially since the Dreyfus affair was still fresh in everyone's imagination; an innocent man had been convicted because of a piece of writing, unsigned and undated. So other traps would be needed.

What made my defense practically useless? In addition to the judges, witnesses, and accusers that had already formed an opinion, you did not help much. I cannot blame you, but this propensity to lie ever since arriving in Paris has led you to be discredited in each of your statements made to the magistrates. The prosecution brought concrete data proving you were not born in the Dutch East Indies or trained by Indonesian priests, that you were not single, and that you had falsified your passport to appear younger. In times of peace, none of this would be taken into account, but inside the War Tribunal you could already hear the sound of bombs brought in by the wind.

So every time I argued something like "She sought out Ladoux as soon as she arrived here," he contested, saying that your only objective was to get more money and seduce him with your charms. This displays unforgivable arrogance; the captain, short and twice your weight, thought you deserved it . . . that you intended to turn him into a puppet in the hands of the Germans. To reinforce that fact, he brought up the zeppelin attack that had preceded your arrival—a failure on the part of the enemy, as it did not hit any strategic location. But for Ladoux, it was evidence that could not be ignored.

You were beautiful, known worldwide, always envied—though never respected—in the concert halls where you appeared. Liars, what little I know of them, are people who seek popularity and recognition. Even when faced with truth, they always find a way to escape, coldly repeating what had just been said or blaming the accuser of speaking untruths. I understand that you wanted to create fantastical stories about yourself, either out of insecurity or your almost visible desire to be loved at any cost. I understand that in order to manipulate so many men, experts themselves in the art of manipulating others, a little fantasy was needed. It's inexcusable, but that is the reality; and that's what led you to where you are now.

I heard you used to say you had slept with "Prince W——," the son of the kaiser. I have my contacts in Germany and all are unanimous that you never came within a hundred kilometers of the palace where he stayed during the war. You boasted you knew many people in the German High Commission; you said it loud enough for all to hear. My dear Mata Hari, what spy in their right mind would mention such barbarities with the enemy? But your desire to call people's attention, at a time when your fame was in decline, only made matters worse.

When you were on the stand, they were the ones who lied, but I was defending a publicly discredited person. From the beginning, the charges listed by the prosecutor are absolutely pathetic, mixing truths you told with lies they decided to interweave. I was shocked when they sent me the material, after you finally understood you were in a difficult situation and decided to hire me.

Here are some of the accusations:

1. Zelle MacLeod belongs to the German intelligence service, where she is known by the name H21. (*Fact.*)

2. She went twice to France since the start of hostilities, surely guided by her mentors, in order to acquire intelligence for the enemy. (*You were followed twenty-four hours a day by Ladoux's men—how could you have done that?*)

3. During her second trip, she offered her services to French intelligence when, in fact, as demonstrated later, she shared everything with German espionage. (*Two mistakes there: You phoned from The Hague to arrange a meeting; this meeting took place with Ladoux on your first trip and absolutely no evidence of secrets "shared" with German intelligence was ever presented.*)

4. She returned to Germany under the pretense of collecting the clothes she had left there, but returned with absolutely nothing and was arrested by British intelligence, accused of espionage. She insisted they get in touch with Captain Ladoux, but he refused to confirm her identity. With no argument or

evidence to stop her, she was dispatched
to Spain and immediately our men saw her
heading to the German consulate. (*Fact.*)

5. Under the pretext of holding confidential
information, she presented herself soon after
at the French consulate in Madrid, saying
she had news of the landing of ammunition
for enemy forces, which was under way
that moment by the Turks and Germans in
Morocco. As we already knew of her role as
double agent, we decided not to risk any man
on a mission that everything indicated was a
trap . . . (*???*)

And so on and so forth; a series of delusional
points not worth enumerating, culminating in the
telegram sent via open channel—or deciphered
code—so as to forever smear a woman who, according to what Kramer later confessed to his interro-
gator, had been *the worst among our poor choices of*
spies to serve our cause. Ladoux even claimed you
had invented the name H21 and your real nom de
guerre was H44, who underwent training in Ant-
werp, Holland, at the famous spy school of Fraulein
Doktor Schragmüller.

In a war, the first casualty is human dignity. Your arrest, as I said before, would serve to show the ability of the French military and divert attention from the thousands of young men dropping dead on the battlefield. In peacetime, no one would accept such delusions as evidence. In wartime, it was all the judge needed to have you arrested the next day.

Sister Pauline, who has acted as a bridge between us, tries to keep me updated on everything that happens at the prison. Once she told me, a little flushed, that she had asked to see your scrapbook with everything that was published about you.

"I was the one who asked. Don't go judging her for trying to scandalize a simple nun."

Who am I to judge? But from this day I have also decided to keep a similar album about you, though I never do that for any other client. As all of France is interested in your case, there is no shortage of news articles about the dangerous spy sentenced to death. Unlike Dreyfus, there is no petition or popular demonstration asking to spare your life.

My album is open next to me, to the page where a newspaper gives a detailed description of what happened the day after the trial. I only found one error in the article, regarding your nationality.

Ignoring the fact that the Third War Council was judging her case at that very moment—or pretending she was not worried about what was happening, since she considered herself a woman above good and evil, always aware of French intelligence's steps—Russian spy Mata Hari went to the Ministry of Foreign Affairs to ask permission to go to the front to meet her lover, whose eyes had been seriously wounded and, even then, was forced to fight. She gave the city of Verdun as her location, a guise meant to show she did not know at all what was happening on the eastern front. She was told that the papers in question had not arrived, but that the minister himself was in charge of it.

The arrest warrant was immediately handed down at

the end of the closed session, which was sealed to reporters. Details of the case will be made known to the public as soon as the trial is over.

The minister of war had issued and sent the arrest warrant three days prior to the military governor of Paris—office 3455 SCR-10—but had to wait until the charge was formalized before such a warrant could be executed.

A team of five people, led by the prosecutor of the Third War Council, went immediately to room 131 of the Hotel Élysée Palace and found the suspect in a silk robe, still taking her breakfast. When asked why she was doing that, she claimed she had had to wake up very early and go to the Ministry of Foreign Affairs and at that moment she was famished.

While they asked the accused to get dressed, they searched the apartment and found a vast amount of material, mostly women's clothing and accessories. Also found were a permit to travel to Vittel and another to perform paid work in France, dated December 13, 1915.

Claiming it was all just a misunderstanding, she demanded they make a detailed list of what they were taking so she could sue them if they did not return everything to her room in perfect condition that same evening.

Only our newspaper had access to what took place at her meeting with the prosecutor of the Third War Council, Captain Pierre Bouchardon, via a secret source who used to provide us with information about the fate of people who had infiltrated and were later unmasked. According to this source—who provided us with the full transcript—Captain Bouchardon handed her the charges hanging over her head and asked her to read them. When she finished, he asked if she wanted a lawyer, which she categorically denied, and answered only:

"But I'm innocent! Someone is joking with me, I work for the French intelligence, when they ask me for something, which has not happened very often."

Captain Bouchardon asked her to sign a document that our source wrote and she did so willingly. She was convinced she would return that same afternoon to the comfort of her hotel and would immediately contact her "immense" circle of friends who would eventually clarify the absurdities of which she was accused.

As soon as she signed the declaration in question, the spy was led directly to Saint-Lazare prison, repeating constantly, already on the verge of hysteria: "I'm innocent! I'm innocent!" while we managed to secure an exclusive interview with the prosecutor.

"She wasn't even a beautiful woman, like everyone claimed," he said. "But her complete lack of scruples, her complete lack of compassion, led her to manipulate and ruin men, leading to at least one suicide. The person standing before me was a spy with her heart and soul."

From there, our team went to the Saint-Lazare prison, where other journalists had already gathered to speak to the director general of incarceration. He seemed to share the opinion of Captain Bouchardon, and also ours, that Mata Hari's beauty had already faded with time.

"Only in her photos is she still beautiful," he said.

"The debauched lifestyle she maintained for so long meant the person who came in here today had huge dark circles under her eyes, hair that was already beginning to discolor at the roots, and very peculiar behavior. She said nothing, except, 'I'm innocent!' always shouting, as if she were back in those days when women, because of their nature, were unable to control their behavior properly. I'm surprised at the bad taste of some friends of mine who had more intimate contact with her."

This was confirmed by the prison doctor, Dr. Jules Socquet, who, in addition to testifying that she was not suffering from any disease—she had no fever, her tongue showed no signs of stomach problems, and auscultation of her lungs and heart showed no suspicious symptoms—released her to be placed in one of the cells of Saint-Lazare after asking the sisters in charge of that wing to provide a stock of sanitary napkins as the prisoner was menstruating.

And it was then, only then, after many interrogations at the hands of the man we call *"Torquemada de Paris,"* that you contacted me and I went to visit you at Saint-Lazare. But it was too late; many of the statements given had already implicated you in the eyes of that man who, as half of Paris knew, had been betrayed by his own wife. A man like that, dear Mata Hari, is like a bloodied beast who seeks revenge instead of justice.

Reading your testimonies before my arrival, I saw you were much more interested in showing your importance than in defending your innocence. You spoke of powerful friends, international success, and crowded theaters, when you should have been doing just the opposite, showing you were a victim, a scapegoat for Captain Ladoux, who had used you in his own internal battle with his fellow colleagues to take over the general management of the counterespionage service.

According to what Sister Pauline told me, when you returned to the cell, you cried incessantly and spent sleepless nights in fear of the mice that infested that infamous prison. Nowadays, it's used only to break the spirits of those who thought they were strong—women like you. She said that the shock of it all would drive you mad before the trial. More than once you asked to be admitted, since you were confined to a solitary cell, with no contact with anyone; the prison hospital, with the little resources it had, would at least allow you to talk to someone.

Meanwhile, your accusers were beginning to get desperate, because they had not found anything among your belongings to incriminate you; the most they found was a leather purse with several business cards. Bouchardon ordered that those respectable gentlemen—who for years begged for your attention—be interviewed one by one, and they all denied any more intimate contact with you.

The arguments of the prosecutor, Dr. Mornet,

bordered on the pathetic. At one point, in the absence of evidence, he claimed:

> "Zelle is the kind of dangerous woman we see nowadays. The ease with which she expresses herself in several languages—especially French—her numerous relations in all areas, her subtle way of worming into social circles, her elegance, her remarkable intelligence, her immorality, all this contributes to her being seen as a potential suspect."

Interestingly, in the end, even Captain Ladoux testified in writing in your favor; he had absolutely nothing to show *Torquemada de Paris*. And he added:

"It is evident she was at the service of our enemies, but you must prove it and I have nothing with me to confirm this statement. If you want vital evidence for questioning, it is better to go to the Ministry of War, which has such documents. For my part, I am convinced that a person who is able to travel during the time in which we live and has contact with so many officers is already proof enough, even though there is nothing in writing or that is not the sort of argument admitted in war tribunals."

I am so tired, I've entered a state of confusion; I think I am writing this letter to you, that I will deliver it to you and we will still have time together to look back, with wounds healed, and be able to, who knows, wipe all of this from our memory?

But in fact, I am writing this for myself, to convince myself that I did everything possible and imaginable; first by trying to get you out of Saint-Lazare; then by fighting to save your life; and finally having the chance to write a book telling the injustice of which you were victim for the sin of being a woman, for the greater sin of being free, for the immense sin of stripping in public, for the dangerous sin of getting involved with men whose reputations needed to be maintained at any cost. This would only be possible if you disappeared forever from France or the world. There is no use describing here the letters and motions I sent to Bouchardon, my attempts to meet with the consul of the Netherlands, nor the list of Ladoux's errors. When the investigation threatened to come to a halt for lack of evidence, Ladoux informed the military governor of Paris that in his possession were several German telegrams—a total of twenty-one documents—that implicated you to the core. And what did these telegrams say? The truth: that you sought out Ladoux when you arrived in Paris, that you were paid for your work, that you demanded more money, that you had lovers in higher circles, but NOTHING, absolutely nothing, that contains any confidential information on our work or the movement of our troops.

Unfortunately, I could not attend all your conversations with Bouchardon, because the criminal "national security law" was enacted, and at many sessions defense lawyers were not allowed—a legal aberration justified in the name of "national security." But I had friends in high places and heard you questioned Captain Ladoux severely, saying you had believed in his sincerity when he offered you money to work as a double agent and spy for France. At this point, the Germans knew exactly what would happen to you, and they also knew all they could do was jeopardize you further. But unlike what's going on in our country, they had already forgotten agent H21 and were focused on stopping the Allied offensive with what really counts: men, mustard gas, and gunpowder.

I know the reputation of the prison where this morning I will visit you for the last time. A former leper colony, then hospice, it was transformed into a place for detention and execution during the French Revolution. Hygiene is virtually nonexistent, the cells are not ventilated, and diseases spread through the fetid air that has no way of circulating. It is basically inhabited by prostitutes and people whose families pull strings to have them removed from their social lives. It also serves for study by physicians interested in human behavior, despite having already been denounced by one of them:

"These young women are of great interest for medicine and moralists—small defenseless creatures who, because of feuding heirs, are sent here at ages as young as seven or eight years old, under the guise of 'parental correction,' spending their childhoods surrounded by corruption, prostitution, and disease, until, when they are released at eighteen, twenty years old, they no longer have the will to live or return home."

Today, one of your cell mates is what we now call a "fighter for women's rights." And what's worse, a "pacifist," "defeatist," "unpatriotic." The charges against Helene Brion, the prisoner to whom I refer, are very similar to yours: receiving money from Germany, corresponding with soldiers and ammunition manufacturers, leading unions, having control of workers, and publishing underground newspapers stating women have the same rights as men.

Helene's fate will probably be the same as yours, though I have my doubts, because she is a French national with influential friends in the newspapers, and did not use the weapon most condemned by all moralists, the one which makes you a favorite to inhabit Dante's Inferno: seduction. Madame Brion dresses as a man and is proud of it. Furthermore, she was judged treasonous by the First War Council, which has a fairer history than the tribunal headed by Bouchardon.

I fell asleep without realizing. I just looked at the clock and there are only three hours to go before I am at that wretched prison for our final meeting. It is impossible to recount everything that has happened since you were forced to hire me against your will. You thought innocence was enough to extract you from the web of the legal system on which we have always prided ourselves, but that in these times of war has become an aberration of justice.

I went to the window. The city is asleep, except for groups of soldiers coming from all over France, singing on their way toward Gare d'Austerlitz, not knowing what fate awaits them. The rumors do not let anyone get any rest. This morning they said they had pushed the Germans beyond Verdun; in the afternoon some alarmist newspaper said Turkish battalions are disembarking in Belgium and moving toward Strasbourg for the final attack. We go from euphoria to despair several times a day.

It's impossible to tell everything that happened from February 13, 1917, when you were arrested, until today, when you will face the firing squad. We will let history do justice to me, to my work. Perhaps one day history might also do justice to you, though I doubt it. You were not merely a person unjustly accused of espionage, but someone who dared to challenge certain customs. And for that you could not be forgiven.

However, one page will suffice to summarize: They attempted to trace the origin of your money, and then that part was sealed as "secret," because they came to the conclusion that many men in high positions would be implicated. Former lovers, without exception, all denied knowing you. Even the Russian with whom you were in love and for whom you were willing to travel to Vittel despite suspicion and risk appeared with one eye still bandaged and read his deposition text in French, a letter read in court with the sole purpose of humiliating you in public. The boutiques where you used to shop were placed under suspicion, and several newspapers made sure to publish your unpaid debts, although you insisted all along that your "friends" had changed their minds about the gifts they'd given you and disappeared without settling anything.

The judges were forced to listen to things from Bouchardon such as: "In the battle of the sexes, all men, no matter their expertise in various arts, are always easily defeated." And he managed to make heard other pearls, such as: "In war, simple contact with a citizen of an enemy country is already suspicious and reprehensible." I wrote to the Dutch consulate asking them to send me some clothes that had been left in The Hague, so you could present yourself with dignity before the court. But to my surprise, despite articles being published fairly often in the newspapers of your country, the government of the Kingdom of the Netherlands was notified of the trial only on the day it began. In any case, it wouldn't have helped; they feared it would affect the "neutrality" of the country.

When I saw you entering the courtroom on

July 24, your hair was unkempt and your clothes faded, but your head was held high and you kept a steady pace, as if you had accepted your fate, refusing the public humiliation to which they wanted to subject you. You understood the battle had come to an end, and that all you could do was leave with dignity. Days earlier, Marshal Pétain ordered the execution of countless soldiers, all accused of treason because they had refused a frontal assault against German machine guns. The French saw in your stance before the judges a way to challenge those deaths and . . .

Enough. There is no use dwelling on something that, I'm sure, will haunt me for the rest of my life. I will lament your departure; I will hide my shame for having erred on some obscure point or for thinking that the justice of war is the same as in peacetime. I will carry this cross with me, but I need to stop scratching the site of infection if the wound is to heal.

However, your accusers will bear much heavier crosses. Though today they laugh and shake hands with one another, the day will come when this entire farce is unmasked. Even if that never happens, they know they condemned an innocent person because they needed to distract the people, just the way our revolution, before bringing about equality, fraternity, and liberty, had to put the guillotine in the public square to provide bloody entertainment to those who still lacked bread. They tied one problem to another, thinking that would result in a solution, but all they did was create a heavy chain of indestructible steel, a chain they will have to drag for the rest of their lives.

There is a Greek myth that has always fascinated me, and that—I think—encapsulates your story. Once there was a beautiful princess who was admired and feared by all because she seemed to be too independent. Her name was Psyche.

Desperate his daughter would wind up a spinster, her father appealed to the god Apollo, who decided to solve the problem: She was to go alone, in mourning dress, to the top of a mountain. Before dawn, a serpent would come to marry her. Intriguing, because in your most famous photo, you have this snake on your head.

But back to the myth: The father did what Apollo ordered, and to the top of the mountain she went. Terrified and freezing cold, she went to sleep, certain she would die.

However, the next day she awoke in a beautiful palace, having been turned into a queen. Each night her husband came to meet her, but he demanded she obey one single condition: to fully trust in him and never see his face.

After a few months together, she was in love with him, whose name was Eros. She loved their conversations, found great pleasure in their lovemaking, and was treated with all the respect she deserved. At the same time, she feared being married to a horrible serpent.

One day, no longer able to control her curiosity, she waited for her husband to fall asleep, gently moved the sheet aside, and with the light of a candle saw the face of a man of incredible beauty. But the light awakened him, and realizing his wife had not been able to be true to his only request, Eros disappeared.

Each time I recall this myth, I wonder: Are we never to be able to see the true face of love? And I understand what the Greeks meant by this: Love is an act of faith and its face should always be covered in mystery. Every moment should be lived with feeling and emotion because if we try to decipher it and understand it, the magic disappears. We follow its winding and luminous paths, we let ourselves go to the highest peak or the deepest seas, but we trust in the hand that leads us. If we do not allow ourselves to be frightened, we will always awaken in a palace; if we fear the steps that will be required by love and want it to reveal everything to us, the result is that we will be left with nothing.

And I think, my beloved Mata Hari, that that was your mistake. After years on the icy mountain, you ended up totally disbelieving in love and decided to turn it into your servant. Love does not obey anyone and will betray those who try to decipher its mystery.

Today you are a prisoner of the French people, but as soon as the sun rises, you will be free. Your accusers will need ever-increasing strength to drag the fetters they forged at your feet in order to justify your death. The Greeks have a word full of contradictory meanings: *metanoia*. Sometimes it means repentance, contrition, confession of sins, the promise not to repeat what we did wrong.

At other times it means going beyond what we know, to stand face-to-face with the unknown, without recollection or memory, without understanding how it will be to take the next step. We are bound to our lives, to our pasts, to the laws of what we consider right or wrong, and suddenly, everything changes. We walk the streets without fear and greet our neighbors, but moments later they are no longer our neighbors—they put up fences and barbed wire so we can no longer see things as they were before. So it will be with me, with the Germans, but above all, with men who decided to find it easier to let an innocent woman die than to recognize their own mistakes.

It is a shame that what happens today already happened yesterday, and will happen again tomorrow; it will continue to happen until the end of time, or until man finds out he is not only what he thinks, but mostly what he feels. The body tires easily, but the spirit is always free and will help us get out, one day, from this infernal cycle of repeating the same mistakes every generation. Although thoughts always remain the same, there is something stronger, and this is called Love.

Because when we truly love, we know others and ourselves better. We do not need words, documents, minutes, statements, accusations, or defenses. We need only what Ecclesiastes says:

> "Instead of justice there was wickedness, instead of righteousness, there was yet more wickedness. . . . But God will judge them all, both the righteous and the wicked, God will judge them both, for there is a time for every intention, a time for every deed."

So be it. Go with God, my beloved.

Epilogue

WOMAN DANCER SHOT BY FRENCH AS SPY

Mlle. Mata-Hari Suffers Penalty for Betraying Secret of 'Tanks' to Germans.

PARIS, Oct. 15.—Mata-Hari, the Dutch dancer and adventuress, who, two months ago, was found guilty by a court-martial on the charge of espionage, was shot at dawn this morning.

The condemned woman, otherwise known as Marguerite Gertrude Zelle, was taken in an automobile from St. Lazaire prison to the parade ground at Vincennes, where the execution took place. Two sisters of Charity and a priest accompanied her.

On October 19, four days after the execution of Mata Hari, her primary accuser, Captain Georges Ladoux, was accused of spying for the Germans and imprisoned. Despite pleading innocence, he was repeatedly questioned by French counterespionage services, although government censorship—legalized during the period of conflict—prevented that fact from being leaked to newspapers. He claimed in his defense that the information had been planted by the enemy:

"It is not my fault that my work left me exposed to any and all sorts of intrigue, while the Germans were collecting data that were essential to the country's invasion." Ladoux was eventually released in

1919, one year after the end of the war, but his reputation as a double agent followed him to the grave.

Mata Hari's body was buried in a shallow grave, which has never been located. According to habits of that time, her head was cut off and handed over to government representatives. For years it was kept in the Anatomy Museum on Rue des Saints-Pères in Paris, until, on an unknown date, it disappeared from the institution. Museum officials only noticed it was missing in the year 2000, although it is believed that Mata Hari's head was stolen well before then.

In 1947, prosecutor André Mornet, by then publicly indicted as one of the lawyers who founded proceedings to revoke the "hasty naturalizations" of Jews in 1940, and largely responsible for the death sentence of the woman he claimed was "the modern-day Salome, whose sole objective is to deliver the heads of our soldiers to the Germans," confided to journalist and writer Paul Guimard that the entire proceedings were based on deductions, extrapolations, and assumptions, concluding with:

"Between us, the evidence we had was so poor that it wouldn't have been fit to punish a cat."

143727

Reply should be addressed to H.M.
Inspector under the Aliens Act,
Home Office, London, S.W., and
the following reference quoted :—

HOME OFFICE.

W.O. 1,101

SECRET
140,193/M.I.5.E.

15th December 1916.

To the Aliens Officer.

Z E L L E, Margaretha Geertruida

Dutch actress, professionally known as MATA HARI.

The mistress of Baron E. VAN DER CAPELLAN, a Colonel in a Dutch Hussar Regiment. At the outbreak of war left Milan, where she was engaged at the Scala Theatre, and travelled through Switzerland and Germany to Holland. She has since that time lived at Amsterdam and the Hague. She was taken off at Falmouth from a ship that put in there recently and has now been sent on from Liverpool to Spain by s.s. "Araguaga", sailing December 1st,

Height 5'5", build medium, stout, hair black, face oval, complexion olive, forehead low, eyes grey-brown, eyebrows dark, nose straight, mouth small, teeth good, chin pointed, hands well kept, feet small, age 39.

Speaks French, English, Italian, Dutch, and probably German. Handsome bold type of woman. Well dressed.

If she arrives in the United Kingdom she should be detained and a report sent to this office.

Former circulars 61207/M.O.5.E. of 9th December, 1915 and 74194/M.I.5.E. of 22nd. February, 1916 to be cancelled.

W. HALDANE PORTER.

H.M. Inspector under the Aliens Act.

Copies sent to Aliens Officers at "Approved Ports" four Permit Offices, Bureau de Controle, New Scotland Yard and War Office (M.I. 5(e)).

Author's Note and Acknowledgments

Although I tried to base my novel on the actual facts of Mata Hari's life, I had to create some dialogue, merge certain scenes, change the order of a few events, and eliminate anything I thought was not relevant to the narrative.

For those who wish to know more about the story of Mata Hari, I recommend Pat Shipman's excellent book *Femme Fatale: Love, Lies and the Unknown Life of Mata Hari* (Harper Collins, 2007); Philippe Collas's *Mata Hari, Sa véritable histoire* (Plon: Paris, 2003)—Collas is the great-grandson of Pierre Bouchardon, one of the characters of this book, and had access to completely new, unpublished material; Frédéric Guelton's "Le dossier Mata Hari," in the *Revue historique des armées*, 247 (2007); and Russell Warren Howe's *"Mournful Fate of Mata Hari, the spy who wasn't guilty"* in Smithsonian Institution, ref. 4224553—among many other articles I used for research. My opening pages are based on the news report filed by Henry G. Wales for the International News Service in October of 1917, and borrow some verbatim language from that report and its retellings.

The Mata Hari file, written up by the British intelligence service, was made public in 1999, and can be accessed on my website in its entirety, or purchased directly in the United Kingdom from the National Archives, reference KV-2-1.

I want to thank my lawyer, Shelby du Pasquier, and his associates for important clarification about the trial; Anna von Planta, my Swiss-German editor, for her rigorous historical review—though we must take into account the main character's tendency to fantasize the facts; and Annie Kougioum, a friend and Greek writer, for her help with the dialogues and weaving the story.

This book is dedicated to J.

A NOTE ON THE TYPE

The text of this book was set in Vendetta, a font designed for Emigre by John Downer and released in 1999. While inspired by fifteenth-century Venetian old style types, Vendetta's character derives from a synthesis of old and new ideas, blending hallmarks of Roman type design with the contemporary concerns of type design in the digital era.

Composed by North Market Street Graphics,
Lancaster, Pennsylvania

Printed and bound by LSC Communications,
Crawfordsville, Indiana

Designed by Cassandra Pappas